I'M THE MAN!!!

R & B's Playhouse Presents "I'm the Man!!!"

Randy E. Thomas I.

 www.trafford.com

North America & international
toll-free: 1 888 232 4444 (USA & Canada)
fax: 812 355 4082

DEDICATION

This book is dedicated to all those who look to make a difference. If we want to change the world around us, we must first change ourselves. If every individual would first worry about themselves, then the outcome of all that is around us will change as well. Psychology teaches; the way we think, dictates how we feel, which dictates how we act. If a person wants to change their actions, they must first change their thought process. We can all make a difference; however, it must be our choice to do so. This book is in memory to all those who lost their lives because of bad choices, either by someone else or by themselves. Let's choose to move forward and make a positive difference.

CONTENTS

CHAPTER 1

FAMILY

Amazing! That's the only way to describe what it's like when you get what you want. Although things in life may not go as one may plan, eating what you want can make even the worst days seem like a blessing. I had the opportunity to have a meal that included only the things I wanted. I got to eat both fried chicken and barbecue ribs, with some macaroni and cheese, corn bread, black eye peas, and peach cobbler for dessert. With all I was dealing with, this meal made me feel like I was truly "The Man!!!"

Life to me was like one of my favorite movies. I enjoyed movies that portrayed a person having nothing, but by the end of the story they had everything they wanted. Two movies that come to mind are Scarface and American Gangster. The star actor in each of these movies began their legacy from the ground up. They started with practically nothing; no power, no money, and no support, but as the story progressed, so did their status.

I was born and raised in Los Angeles, California in a small town called Carson. Carson was established to be a new upcoming middle class city in the midst of Compton and Long Beach. Compton was known for poverty, crime, drugs, gang related activities, and everything negative a person could imagine. Living conditions were tough due to so much poverty and the high demand for increased personal needs. The negative attitude people had towards Compton, overflowed into other cities such as Watts, East Los Angeles, Wilmington, and so on. Since these cities were also culturally stereotype, due to the background of those living within its borders, many individuals faced unfair disadvantages in education and decent employment.

Carson was created to help change people's view of the negativity that was already engrained. There were hotels chains, parks for families to bring their children and pets to, new schools to eliminate busing students to the already crowded schools in the afore mentioned cities, a shopping mall and many other amenities to create a more positive community. A few major companies established home offices within the city as well. I guess the land was cheap and maybe the companies saw it as a financial opportunity, while at the same time providing a positive outlook for the newly established city. The idea of creating such a place was very positive and uplifting; therefore, it was safe to say that its creators were on the right track.

Our family was the typical two incomes, low educated, struggling minority family, trying to achieve the "American Dream." My father, Earle Johnson, worked as a manual laborer. He loaded and unloaded cargo trains. He worked the night shift from midnight to 8:00 o'clock in the morning. Although this job kept him in great physical condition, it didn't take a genius to do what he did. He worked hard and many times he worked alone, having no one to communicate with for long periods of time during his shifts. I guess that's why my father appeared to be quiet and isolated, because that's how he spent most of his time while at work, which was sometimes six days a week. He was not as active as my mom was when it came to church; however, he was raised believing in God.

My mother, Dianne Johnson, worked as a secretary for one of those large companies that moved into our neighborhood. She worked more traditional hours, like 9 to 5, five days a week. She spent a lot of time taking verbal abuse from bosses that had little to no respect for her services; however, she didn't let that affect who and what she was. She was a God fearing woman who put her faith and trust in who she considered to be the only form of hope for our future. She was an active participant in the church and was there every time the doors appeared to open. As a child she was raised going to church; therefore, as an adult she tried to keep the same tradition for her family. I can remember spending a lot of my time with both her and my siblings at church. To be honest, it wasn't as bad as some people may think.

There were four kids in our family. The oldest was my brother Earle Jr., who was named after our father. We called him "Ditto" for short because he was almost an exact duplicate of our dad. He was a star athlete and could play just about any sport; however, his love was football. He played on both the offensive and defensive side of the ball. He also was a better than average student, even though he did not always give school his best efforts. My brother was about ten years older than me, so we really didn't spend much quality time together. His life was more about girls and sports, which I didn't fit into either at the time.

My sisters, Natalie and Nicole were twins and they were about eight years older than me. They were very attractive and popular; therefore, they received a lot of attention from everybody. As students, they were always near the top of their class and they were also cheerleaders. My relationship with them was similar to that of my brother, due to our age difference. Their interest centered on their appearance and cheerleading. That meant everything to them. They were always doing their hair, make-up, and practicing cheers.

I can remember my mother yelling at them because everything was about their physical looks. If it wasn't for them having good grades, one would think that they were very shallow. My father would always have to tell them to put more clothes on and wash some of that circus stuff off their faces. He hated to see his girls flaunt themselves as they did, but they were young and that's what was important to them. We really didn't have much of a closeness, the only time I really spent with them was during meal times and in the car going to church.

I was the baby in the family and nobody called me by my real name, which was William Earle. They all called me Pee-Wee. Being the baby was difficult because I was always being told what to do, when to do it, and how to do it. I was the last person to get anything; last to get food, to get new clothes, even to get attention. I wasn't involved in sports like my brother, but I did like to play things every now and then. I was an alright student, but like most boys I didn't try as hard as I should have. My favorite thing to do was sit back and watch movies and trust me, I did a lot of that.

The worst time of my life came when I was about nine years old. My father was standing on a corner talking with some friends after work. While they were minding their own business, a drive by shooter passed and shot at all of them. Two guys were hit in the arm, another guy was hit in the leg, yet my father was hit twice in the head. There was another guy with them, but he didn't get hit at all. My father was pronounced dead immediately. The only good thing was that he didn't suffer. The shooter was never found; therefore, no fault was labelled for his death.

Of course, my mother took the death of my father harder than anyone else. He was her lover, her friend, and her partner. With his passing, she now had to play the role of both mom and dad. She continued to work as a secretary and tried to keep the family moving forward as best she could. Through our tough experiences it felt like every time we took one step forward, it would force us two steps back. Due to my mom's belief, she always made the comment to us that "God will provide."

Although my mom was always at church, through my eyes things seemed to get worse and worse. We were in high demand of many immediate needs. We had financial needs, physical needs, and psychological needs. Any need you could think of; I am sure it defined what our family was hurting to have. The church tried to help us because that's what they do; however, it didn't feel right. I remember once when Sister Jones and a couple of other members came to the house. It was sometime shortly after my father's funeral, they brought us some food. As good and loving as that sounds, it felt weird because they kept asking questions as if we were being interrogated. They would ask whether or not my mom spent time crying a lot, whether or not she was able to provide enough food, and whether or not she appeared depressed. Although these questions represented concern and love for someone, I felt as if they were being nosey and trying to get into our business.

I would like to believe that my brother and sisters were highly effected by the loss of our father; however, their actions seemed to show that they were so caught up in their own lives, that they didn't have time to stop and worry about the down fall of our family. One morning I was feeling sick and extremely sad about my father, but my brother was eager to play in his football game that evening and my sisters were making themselves pretty for a pep-rally at school. They made such a big deal about their own activities, my mom got so caught up in their fun that she forgot about me not feeling well.

My mom was running behind them so much, trying to help prepare the things they needed that I felt completely invisible. Since my siblings were in high school, they needed to be out of the house at least an hour or so before me. As I remained in my room, I heard everyone walk out of the house. I sat there waiting for someone to come back in and say something to me. After about ten minutes had passed, I realized that everyone had forgotten about me. It didn't bother me that my siblings didn't say anything, but I was crushed that my mom failed to acknowledge me. Experiences such as this occurred time and time again.

I may not expect much from my brother and sisters, but I did expect a lot from my mom and during that time in my life, I felt left out. The multiple experiences of feeling invisible led me to believe that if I meant more, then everyone would prioritize my needs. In order to mean more I needed to increase my importance, my popularity, my worth, and my respect. I needed to become what I believed to be "The Man."

CHAPTER 2

DESTRUCTION

"We are gathered here to pay respect and lay to rest our brother Earle Johnson," the minister said as he presided over my father's funeral. "He was a Christian, a husband, a father, and a friend. Although we may feel that Earle was taken from us prematurely, our schedule is not always the same as His schedule, our desires are not always His desires and our will is not always His will."

As the minister spoke, tears ran down the faces of almost everyone in attendance. As I sat there looking at my father's body, I could remember both the good and bad times we had together. Overall, I truly loved my father and it was going to be difficult dealing with his absence.

"To see death when it wasn't being chased. To experience disaster while being peaceful. To face destruction while all appears to be normal. These are situations that no one should ever have to face; however, you are our God and all things work together for the good of those that love the Lord." As the minister continued to stress the unfairness of what we were dealing with, he always added that this is what God desires.

As the funeral ended, I can remember thinking that things were going to get a lot worse before they got better. I can recall my mother trying to be strong throughout the service; however, as they lowered my father into the grave, she could not hold back her emotions anymore. She started crying uncontrollably and collapsed to the ground. While people hurried to her aid, I could see the faith our family once had drift away from the hearts of all of us. My brother and sisters were extremely emotional and people were trying to console them, yet I was frozen. It really was not all that clear to me what was actually going on, but I knew it was very bad.

Death was something new for me; therefore, the understanding of my father never coming back was not as clear as it was for the rest of my family. I knew he was dead, but I didn't quite understand what that meant, as life continued for the rest of us. While attending to my mother and my siblings, the congregation started to sing one of the songs my father would sing, on the rare occasions when he would attend church and lead singing. The song was entitled Mansion, Robe, and a Crown:

I'm gonna trade my earthly home, for a better one bright and fair.

Christ left to prepare a mansion, for his children in the air.

I'll join him in that land where tears, no sorrows can be found.

When I receive a mansion (mansion), robe and crown…

This song was so powerful and to hear the congregation sing it with the passion and emotions they were feeling at that time, it sounded heavenly. The song has three tear jerking verses that tell a hopeful story, along with a chorus that separates the voices of both the men and women. As the third verse was completed, the song leader led the chorus four more times. I must say, it was a very beautiful song. It was the perfect fit for the situation.

As sad and angry as the service made me feel, both the song and what followed after the final prayer were two things that bought about great joy for me. In our culture, what followed was some good eating. The food that was available was practically all of my favorites. We had an endless amount of fried chicken and barbeque ribs. There were multiple salads: green salads, potato salads, pasta salads, as well as macaroni and cheese dishes. We had sweet yams, corn, beans, and a lot of vegetables. The food tables seemed to go on forever, which was perfect for me because I loved to eat.

After dinner, the desserts were a perfect topping and conclusion to our festival in remembrance of my father. We had sweet potato pie, peach cobbler, red velvet cake, every assortment of cookies possible, bread and banana pudding, and like the food, that list went on and on as well. I believe that people prepare such a spread of food at funerals to provide those grieving an opportunity to put their pain aside, if only for a short period of time.

I still think about the ride home from the funeral, it was extremely quiet. My mom didn't even turn on the radio and no one asked her to either. It was so quiet that I could almost hear my own heartbeat. When we arrived at the house, my mom went straight to her bedroom and closed the door. We figured she wanted to be alone, so none of us bothered her.

My siblings and I stayed in the living room. This was one of the few times we actually spent time together. None of us wanted to be alone, so we all remained in the same room. After about ten minutes of quietness, my brother asked me if I understood what was going on. My look of blankness was answer enough. As an older sibling should, my brother began to explain to me what the reality of today was about.

"Death is the end of one's life here on earth," he explained. "Remember how in church they always talk about Heaven?" he asked. I never said a word, I just shook my head responding yes. "Dad is in Heaven, he's living with God and all the people we read about in the bible."

Although my brother appeared to be calm as he spoke to me, I could see that he was suffering. He sat on the couch with his hands clinched and his legs rocking back and forth. My sisters just sat quietly, which was strange because they were always talking. Everything was weird, so I just stayed quiet as my brother kept speaking.

"Dad is walking in Heaven on those streets pathed of gold and singing endless praises. He's flying around from cloud to cloud with his angel wings and chilling in his mansion."

My brother was actually doing everything he could to put me at ease. He even stood up and walked to where I was sitting, put his arm around me and ended his comforting speech with, "he's getting everything ready for us, whenever our time comes to go home."

My brother and I had never had a moment such as the one we were having at that time. Whether he knew it or not, I greatly appreciated what he was doing. I was still unable to cry because I couldn't get passed being angry at God for taking my father. My dad spent a lot of his time giving. He worked hard trying to provide a better life for his family and he seemed to be a good Christian man, even though he did not attend church as much as my mom would have liked him to.

Based on the things my brother said about my dad's current situation, him walking on streets of gold, him chilling in a mansion, and him flying with his angel wings, he is now "The Man." My problem with all that was why he had to die in order to become "The Man?" What good is it to be the Christian people talk about and then have to go through what my father did, yet when you die, everything is perfect?

Constantly thinking about my father's funeral made me realize that I did not want to live and die like him, and then finally become "The Man." It was at that point, I decided that I wanted to be "The Man" while I was still alive.

CHAPTER 3

MONEY TALKS

L ife is about the choices we make and the opportunities we take advantage of; however, those outcomes usually make more sense when one looks back on their actions. Older people always express to younger generations to think before we act, yet we tend to fall into the attitude of, let's see what happens. Our outcomes generally define who and what we become.

The number one thing that all powerful people have is money. At the age of nine, how could I get my hands on enough money to create the power I wanted? I knew my success wouldn't happen overnight, so I needed to map out a long term plan to create a solid foundation. The question that kept running around my mind, was what could I do to build the success I wanted? For days I kept trying to think of a plan, until it finally hit me. Kids of all ages, creed, and color enjoy candy. If candy is the demand, then I'll need to provide the supply. I'll become the candy man and sell it for a profit. I can sell paydays, snickers, skittles, milky ways, and many other famous candies. The reality is that kids will buy whatever candy I have.

The first thing I needed to do was figure out how to get my hands on some candy. The problem was, I did not have any money. The only way I could start this successful train was to get my hands on as much candy as I could, so I could establish a consistent income.

Early one Saturday morning, I went to the gas station near my house. I knew there was only one or two people working, so I waited before going into the store area for a few customers to walk inside. My plan was to buy one item and at the same time fill my pockets up with as many candy bars as I could. Since this was my first time trying to take something, it took me a little longer to get started with my plan. I walked around the store for about ten minutes, as people came in and left the store area. At one point, one of the attendants asked me if I needed any help. I got so scared, that I finally ran out of the store.

By leaving the store it made it impossible for me to go back without the attendants being suspicious. I sat on the curve mentally beating myself up because I couldn't follow through with my plan. I sat there trying to motivate myself for about twenty minutes, until I went across the street to another gas station. As I walked inside, there were a number of customers both shopping and standing in line. I figured it was going to be easier to get what I wanted because there was no way the attendants could watch everything. I quickly grabbed six candy bars and thrusted them into my jacket pocket. As I stood in line waiting to pay for the gum I was actually buying, my heart began beating like a drum.

"Next in line," the attendant yelled in order for customers to hear him over all the noise that was in the store area.

The problem was, I couldn't move. My feet where stuck in cement shoes and my legs would not allow me to go forward.

"Next in line young man," the attendant said again.

As I moved slowly to the window, the attendant starred at me intensely. I knew I was caught, but it was too late to run. When I finally made it to the window, I placed the gum on the counter.

"Is that all?" the attendant asked.

Once again, I knew I was in trouble because he must have known that I had more candy on me. I just starred at the attendant while holding a dollar bill in my hand.

"You going to give me the money or what?" the attendant asked.

I couldn't believe how scared I was. When the attendant asked me again for the money, that's when I started to believe that I might actually get away with the stolen candy in my pocket. With all that, I still could not move to pay for my gum. As fear had completely taken over my body, an older lady at the cashier next to me, grabbed my gum and asked the attendant to add it to her bill. She noticed the fear in me and said don't worry son, this is a treat from me to you. I said thanks, grabbed the gum and ran out of the store.

After running almost all the way home, I stopped to empty my pockets. I had stolen two snickers, two paydays, and two butterfingers. The gum was mine, but since someone else paid for it, I would be able to sell it for a profit as well. Since I loved candy, the difficult thing for me was not to eat any of it, but save it and sell it at school. My plan was to sell the candy to students who would rather spend money on candy than on school food, which was everyone. The thought was, they could eat food when they got home from school.

Later that evening, my mom needed to go to the grocery store to pick up food for the week, since nobody was home, I had to go with her. The adrenalin was still at a high level in my body, so I looked at this as another opportunity to get more candy. On the entire drive to the grocery store I couldn't stop thinking about the money I was going to make from what I already had. My plan was to sell the candy bars for $1 dollar each, which meant I would make $7 dollars. Right then, I decided that I wanted to make more money; therefore, I needed to get additional bars of candy. My goal was to find a reason to separate from my mom, so I could get the additional bars when we got to the grocery store. The only question I had from that point was how and when I was going to get away, so I could execute my plan.

As we entered into the store, I asked my mom if we needed any bread. As she looked at her list, she told me yes, so I offered to go and get it for her. Since the candy bars were near the cash registers, I got the bread first and while on my way back I grabbed five candy bars. I stuffed four of them into my pocket and asked my mom to buy the one bar I showed her. Since I assisted her with getting the bread, she agreed to purchase the candy. I took advantage of the opportunity and offered to help out with additional products. I got toilet paper, milk, cheese, and lunch snacks as well. I was creating a pattern for the next time we came to the grocery store. When we finished our shopping and got in line to pay for our groceries, a manager walked up to us.

"How are you doing today?" he asked.

My mom responded with a simple hello and we're doing fine. I couldn't speak because in my mind, I was caught again.

"I saw you running around, were you helping get stuff for your mom?" he said as he turned towards me.

I knew for a fact that I was in trouble, but my mom quickly jumped in and responded to him with a simple, "Yes he was!" She went on to say, "My little man was a big help today and for his efforts I'm getting him some candy.

Based on my fear always taking over whenever I felt busted, I realized that I had to do a better job at controlling my emotions, just like I did at the funeral. This was the second time that someone had to save me from giving myself away. Although I got away with getting the candy, I did not do as well as I thought I would, I just got lucky.

Aside from the bars I got earlier, now I had two crunch bars and two more snicker bars. The extra bar, I used as a reward, and of course it was a payday, which is my favorite.

When we finally got home, I told my mom I needed to go to the restroom. I used that as a divergent so I could once again empty the bars out of my pocket. While in my room, I put the new bars in my book bag along with the other ones I got earlier. I quickly ran to the bathroom and flushed the toilet to give the appearance that I actually used it. I was so excited about my business getting started that the expression on my face was like a kid on Christmas morning.

When I finally made it back to the car to help my mom she asked, "What's up with you?"

I responded by saying nothing, but kept unloading the car. People always say that moms can tell when something is up with their kids. She may not have known what actually was going on, but she could tell something was happening. After helping with the groceries, I even started helping her with preparing dinner.

After dinner and a couple of television shows, it was time for me to go to bed. As I got myself prepared, the excitement of going to school in the morning was higher than it had ever been. The night felt like an eternity because all I could think about was selling my candy and making money. I guess you could say I was like a kid on Christmas morning, as described earlier, I could not sleep. The night appeared to drag on with no end in sight. I walked to the bathroom on three different occasions, trying to do anything to kill time.

Without notice, I feel asleep because the next thing I knew, my mom was waking me up.

"Get up, it's time to get ready for school," she said.

I wiped my eyes with my hands and jumped out of the bed. As I got cleaned up and dressed, my thoughts were all about selling candy and making what I considered to be, big money.

When I arrived at school, I quickly ran to my friends on the playground under the tree where we always met. Instead of waiting until lunch time, I offered to sell candy to them, then and there. Well, just as I figured, they were willing and able to buy. I made $6 off of them alone. I had five bars left and of course word got around. Before recess, I had sold everything. I actually had $11 dollars in my pocket and had to tell people I was out. It felt bad saying "no" to people because that meant I was passing up on making more money.

I knew I needed to find a way to get more candy. I couldn't make it with just ten or so bars, I needed to get my hands on a larger amount. I couldn't keep going to the same stores because eventually they would catch on to what I was doing and I would get into big trouble; therefore, I had to create a new plan.

I was able to go to different stores about two to three times a week to get anywhere from 15 to 20 bars of candy, which calculated to the same amount of dollars each week. A kid my age having $15 to $20 dollars a week meant a lot. This routine went on for about a month. One day, while on my way to get more candy, the delivery schedule of a couple of stores caught my attention. Large delivery trucks were bringing candy to various stores. I monitored those delivery schedules for about two weeks. Eventually, it was time to make my move. With the skills I had developed over the past number of weeks, I knew I'd be able to get at least one box per truck.

Early one Saturday morning, I snuck out of the house and watched one of those delivery trucks as it arrived at the store I was monitoring. At this stage in my business, I didn't have the same fear I had when I started. As soon as the delivery guy loaded his cart and entered into the store, I quickly jumped into the truck and found a box of snickers. I put the box in my back pack and ran out of that truck like a mother lion running after a breakfast meal. When I got back home, I had to sneak back into the house. This time it was harder because my brother and sisters were awake. I was able to crawl through the bathroom window and run across the hall into my room. When I opened up the box I saw that it contained 50 bars of candy. Immediately, with at least two boxes a week my income would increase by five times the amount I was used to getting. Just like that, my profits, power, and popularity would increase greatly.

My goal was to go out once on Saturday morning and then again on Wednesday morning before school and duplicate the same process. To make this really work, I needed to get the schedule of other trucks. I didn't want the trucks I was taking from to catch on to my plan, just like my fear of going to the same stores when I first started this business. The success of my business adventure was amazing. I was making money and in some cases, I was trading candy for favors and various other things. This process went on for about two years. Although I could not set up a bank account, I was able to hide the money in an empty leg of my bed. I knew some day it would get filled up, but for now that hiding spot would have to do.

At my age, I had money, respect, a lot more friends, and many favors that I could cash in on at any given time. It was safe to say that I was well on my way to becoming what I defined as "The Man."

CHAPTER

4

EXAM ADVENTURE

The hardest thing about having money, was keeping it hidden. By hiding your money, nobody knows what you have, especially if you're not supposed to have it in the first place. I guess it's like winning the lottery, although you want to keep your new finances a secret, how you live your new life style could be a dead give-a-way. The money I was making was nothing close to winning the lottery; however, it was a great deal for someone of my age.

I've been selling candy and whatever else I could get my hands on for the past two years. Although I was getting tired with the efforts of getting candy on a weekly base, I love money. I was making an average of just over $100 dollars a week. For an adult, that's nothing, but for a child around my age, it was a great deal of money. Although I had been doing the candy thing for a while, I was ready for something new. Even though I kept doing the candy business, my concern was about starting a new adventure. Just as I asked myself when I started the candy business, what would kids be willing to buy with their allowance, their birthday money, their lunch money, and even money they would take?

I spent a number of days contemplating my next business adventure. It wasn't until I was sitting in class taking a test when the answer came to me. I hated studying for exams, yet I always wanted and needed to do well. What if I could get a copy of the exams my teachers gave before the actual test day? I would satisfy my goal of not wanting to study and at the same time satisfy my mom by getting good grades. It appeared to me to be a win-win business.

At this stage in life, school really wasn't a priority for me or my friends. My thought process was that many kids my age felt the same way. If I could relieve students of the stress of studying, it would make young people feel more positive about themselves because it would get parents off their backs. I truly believe that kids would pay almost anything to get their hands on teacher's exams. The only problem I needed to solve was finding out where my teachers kept their exams.

Knowing what to do and how to do it are two different things. I needed to get my hands on the exams early enough, so I could offer them to students, leaving them enough time to prepare. The two biggest concerns I had was not getting caught while getting the exams and not having students talk too much about having them before the actual test dates. The ability to control both concerns would mean a great deal of money to me and if successful, this business could last for a long time.

It was best for me to start monitoring my own teachers first, before focusing on any other teachers. I needed to figure out where they kept their work, then I had to create a plan to get it without their knowledge. My first choice was Mrs. Johnson, my science teacher. She was a perfect choice because she was new to our school; therefore, she had no previous knowledge of anyone or anything. Mrs. Johnson carried a lunch to school and ate in her class every Monday through Thursday; however, on Friday's she left the school grounds and was gone for about thirty minutes. After monitoring Mrs. Johnson for a couple of weeks, it was obvious that she was the best choice to begin my new business adventure. When she left school for those thirty minutes, the back window of her classroom was open and her materials were stored in the second drawer of her desk.

While watching Mrs. Johnson, I also picked up on the habits of Mrs. Hernandez, my math teacher and Mr. Jenkins a history teacher. Mr. Jenkins was not one of my current instructors, but he was my teacher from a previous class. After following those teachers for another few weeks, it was time to execute my plan.

The next Friday, I prepared to pull off a hockey "hat trick." My intentions were to get exams from all three teachers I had been monitoring. Mrs. Johnson was my first victim. As lunch began, I watched her drive out of the parking lot. I was able to get into her class through the back window that was open. Once I got into her classroom, the drawer was unlocked where she kept the materials for our class. I was able to get a snap shot of four different exams. Mrs. Hernandez's room was connected to Mrs. Johnson's room; therefore, all I needed to do was go through their connecting door. The hallway doors were locked when classes were out, but the interior connecting doors were always open. I was able to find Mrs. Hernandez's materials in a locked cabinet. Getting past the lock was no big deal, but finding all her test for the term was more of a struggle. Once I found them, I got snap shots of those as well.

My operation ended as the first bell sounded letting us know that we had five more minutes before lunch was over. Due to the loss of time, I was unable to complete the "hat trick" I wanted. I was unable to make an attempt at getting into Mr. Jenkins's class, so I just saved it for another date. I was able to secure ten different exams between Mrs. Johnson and Mrs. Hernandez; therefore, this was still a great start to my new business.

The first exam of the two teachers was Mrs. Hernandez. Her math exam was scheduled for Thursday, two weeks from now. This meant that I had nine days before show time. Since Mrs. Hernandez was my math instructor, I would be the first client to test the validity of what I was selling; however, due to my desire of wanting money and power, I could not let the opportunity of having an exam go by without selling it to a few other people.

There were still two problems I needed to be aware of in reference to my business, one was whom do I offer the exams to and the other was how to prevent people from spreading the word of what I was doing. I didn't want information about my business getting to the wrong ears. The only answer to both of those questions was to deal only with individuals I considered to be friends. Those are people who would love to take advantage of the opportunity to increase their grades, without actually doing more work and without jeopardizing the good thing they had. Students who tend to fit that description were generally athletes and other popular individuals. After considering all things, I decided to offer the first exam to ten students. Five of those students were in my class and the other five had Mrs. Hernandez at a different time.

We finally made it to the end of the week, which was Friday. I approached Justin, who was a friend of mine and he played on the baseball team. Justin was an average student and didn't push himself to achieve much more than an average grade, which kept him eligible to play on the team. I figured he was a great candidate for taking advantage of my exam business. After explaining to him the possibility of having access to the following week's exam, he jumped at the offer. The agreement was for $5 dollars and he couldn't say anything to anyone. Things went so well with Justin, that I continued the same sells pitch to a few other people I trusted. I received commitments from the ten people I spoke to and they assured me that they would have the money I required by the following Monday. It was then that I agreed to get each of them a copy of the exam. Although I could have made more money, I wanted to make sure of the success of my plan before kicking it into high gear.

When Monday arrived it was money time. I had instructed the students to meet me on the field and I would give them a copy of the answers. I did not want the actual test floating around, because somehow, someone might allow it to become more public then I wanted it to be. This would kill my business, which means it would eliminate my money.

As I gave the answers to each student, I also informed them not to get everything right because it would throw up red flags. Since these chosen few were considered average students, a perfect score would alert the teacher that something was going on. Each individual claimed to understand my concern and admitted that they would miss a few questions to ensure continued business. That morning I made $50 dollars, but if everything works out as I planned, I should be able to earn two to three times that amount moving forward.

This same routine went on for the next few months in both Mrs. Hernandez and Mrs. Johnson's classes. I was also able to get exams for Mr. Jenkins, Mr. Jones and Mrs. Rodriguez. With so many exams, there were times I had to let the reality of people run its course. I had to tell customers that I didn't have certain test. Since my customer base continued to grow, teachers were experiencing a great increase in the average scores on the test they were administering. I know teachers believe they have the ability to educate, motivate, and encourage students; however, the increase in grades had nothing to do with what teachers believed. At this stage in life, I feel that students can care less about that crap. All they cared about was that they were making better grades and both teachers and parents were happy. For me, I was making good money and in my mind, providing a beneficial service.

As I walked through the halls, students of all backgrounds were acknowledging me. The athletes were giving me high fives, the popular kids were including me in their involvements, and the smart students welcomed me in as well, since my grades were now, just like theirs. It was safe to say, I was well on my way to becoming "The Man!"

CHAPTER

5

COMPROMISE

For the past couple of years, business has been going extremely well. Between both my candy, which I have decreased somewhat, and exam selling operation, I was averaging just over $1000.00 dollars a month. It's safe to say that the hallow leg of my bed had filled up and it was time to put my money in another location. Although business was going well and word of mouth was traveling fast, my family was still unaware of what was happening in my life. Maybe my brother and sisters knew, but it wasn't important enough to concern themselves with. They had their own lives to deal with and the things that were important to them had nothing to do with me.

One Saturday morning, while I was playing basketball at the park with some of my friends, it became obvious that rumors of my success in business had reached the ears of some important people. As my friends and I were getting a drink from the water fountain, we were approached by some members of the West DA Boys.

The West DA Boys were a well-known gang that basically ran all the illegal activities in our neighborhood. As the guys surrounded us at the water fountain, one of them spoke, "we understand that you've created a very lucrative business and someone wants to speak with you about your success."

We all knew who that someone was and how dangerous he was, but since my friends were with me, I wasn't too worried. Just then the guys motioned for my friends to leave because they only wanted to deal with me. That's when it got a little scary.

"We've been watching you," another one of the members said. "You've been selling stolen candy and teacher's exams for the past few years."

"…and your success has been well documented by our gang," one of the other guys stated.

Since the gang members were just talking to me, I concluded that they were not going to attack or rob me. I assumed they just wanted to know how I ran my business.

"Over the past number of years that you've been running your business, about how many customers do you think you've developed?" One of the guys asked.

I honestly didn't have a clue of how many clients I had, so I answered by telling them I didn't know, but the number had to be pretty large.

Whether the guys were satisfied or not with my answer, I didn't know, but the one that appeared to be the leader stepped closer to me.

"We know you play basketball here almost every Saturday morning," he said in a whisper. "Next week, Big O will meet with you to discuss some future arrangements; therefore, make plans on being here." After those words, all four guys walked away.

I stood there frozen like a bump on a log. Big O was the leader of the West DA Boys and his history was well known around our hood. I didn't know what his plan was for me, but I'm sure my life and my business were about to change in a major way.

With this suspected change, one of my fears was about to be challenged. As much as I wanted to become "The Man," I wasn't ready for my family to find out about my involvements. My mom was busy trying to keep things with the family going, due to the absence of my father. If she knew what I was doing, she would punish me like never before. Part of that punishment would possible be not letting me out of her sight, ever! My brother was preparing to head off for his senior year of university life and my sisters were working and more concerned about making it through their last year of community college. Although my family had their own lives to live, if they had a clue about my activities, I would become a higher priority to them, but not in a good way.

That Friday night before the meeting with Big O, I could not sleep. I stayed awake over half the night. I wondered about the plan that Big O wanted to discuss with me. Some of the thoughts that went through my head were if he wanted to take some of the money from my businesses; was he going to ask me to join their gang and then take all my money; or was he going to put an end to what I created? I didn't have any idea of what was going to happen, but one thing I was sure of was that this meeting was a compliment to what I was doing. The West DA Boys had their dirty hands in everything and I created something that caught their attention. Thinking like that made me feel a little more at ease because I had proven that I had the ability of becoming "The Man!"

I woke up earlier than usual and headed to the park to play some basketball and to have my meeting with Big O. As I was walking to meet up with my friends, two guys jumped me from behind the bushes alongside the houses across the street from the park. They grabbed me and covered my head. Then they tossed me into the back of a flatbed truck. At first I was scared, but when I realized what was happening, I calmed down. I figured it had to be the West DA Boys. They more than likely had been following me from the time I left my house.

The ride was short. It took less than five minutes to get to where ever it was we were going. As the truck stopped, two guys helped me to my feet and assisted me out of the truck.

"What up little homey, you good?" A voice asked. Since I was still under the cover that they placed on my head, I didn't know who was talking; however, I answered simply by saying "I'm good."

The person continued speaking by saying, "we understand that you've been doing very well with your businesses. You've been taking candy and then selling it for pure profit. You've been taking exams from teachers and selling them as well," the person said in a congratulatory voice. "If I'm correct, you've been in business for just over four years, which means you have a great base of customers," the secret person stated.

By this time, I figured the person speaking was Big O; therefore, I made it a point to show the highest level of respect. "Yes sir!" I responded.

"Our interest is not in your business; however, we want to help add to the success you've created," the voice expressed.

To me it sounded like I would have a chance to make more money, but this time with a well-known partner. As dangerous as this sounded, I got into business to make money and generate power, so why stop or run when a greater opportunity presents itself? In a calm yet adventures voice, I responded by saying, "I'm good with the chance to add to my success."

With my approval of wanting to increase success, the bag was removed from my head.

"My name is Big O and I'm glad you have decided to partner up with the West DA Boys," the revealed mystery voice said. "All you have to do is start out providing your customers with this little bag, which includes two samples of what we call "tick-tacks."

As I looked at the bag, the little pill really looked like a "tick-tack," but I am sure it was not a breath mint. I asked Big O what the "tick-tack" actually was.

"This is actually a combination of stimulant drugs, that when dissolved in a person's system, allows them to feel as if they were on cloud nine," he responded. "The key thing about this product, is that it is an untraceable drug; therefore, doctors and police officers can't diagnose its affects with absolute assuredness." As Big O continued speaking, he was given a brown paper bag from one of the guys standing behind him. "In this bag you have twenty little bags, each containing two "tick-tacks." Give a bag to each of your favorite customers and ask for their opinion on its effects."

This was not a game anymore, once I accepted these bags, the consequences of my actions increased greatly. My continued success would have an extremely high financial benefit, yet if I get caught, the punishment would be a lot worse than just getting caught taking candy and teacher's exams.

Big O informed me that after I finish giving out all twenty bags, he'll give me twenty more for the purpose of selling? Each bag would contain two "tick-tacks" and would cost $5 dollars. From the sale of each bag, I would make $1 dollar. Big O strongly encouraged me not to carry all the bags at one time because I was financially responsible if any of them were lost or stolen. He also informed me that if I brought any kind of trouble to him or his gang, my family would suffer the wrath of the West DA Boys. Before they sent me on my way with my first twenty bags, Big O expressed that prior to giving out "tick-tacks," let customers know, "Don't step up unless you're ready to stand up!" Both Big O and his boys started laughing as they led me on my way.

With all that had just happened, I completely forgot about playing basketball and started heading home. My concern was no longer only about my business, but now about my partnership and responsibilities to the West DA Boys. As dangerous and rewarding as my endeavors could be, again one of my largest concerns was about keeping my actions away from my family. Like any parent, if my mom knew what I was doing, she'd kill me. For me, I needed this opportunity if I wanted to achieve my goal at becoming "The Man,"

CHAPTER 6

A NEW ADVENTURE

I was ordered to wear a particular uniform, which I would not have chosen if given the opportunity to decide; however, in certain situations one has no say. Sometimes you have to do as instructed.

It felt like a long time coming, but high school finally opened its doors to me. Although I was beginning my life as a freshman, I wasn't going to be at the bottom of the totem pole. Due to my past business experiences and my new business partner, my popularity was sure to skyrocket to the top. My plan for the first few days of school was to scout out teachers for my exam business and to reunite with customers who may be potential clients for my new endeavor with the West DA Boys.

I never really dealt with upper classmen, but due to my new business partner, it was not going to be too difficult having to approach them. My plan was to see if students were still on board with my exam business and then see who was willing to try my new involvement. Although I did not have any products on me, since I left them at home, I did promise that I would have samples by the end of the week. My main focus for this new business would be the athletes. Due to their popularity and their possible knowledge of Big O, they would be a great pathway to initiate my "tick-tack" adventure and to open the doorway to many more customers. All of this represents the outcome of why I got into business in the first place, which is money!

Being in high school was a far different animal, compared to when I attended middle school. The students were bigger, things moved a lot faster, and the number of students was more than triple the size from middle school. These facts may appear negative; however, what they really represented was an increased opportunity. With a greater demand for business, it also meant a higher level of risk.

When Friday arrived, I was extremely excited because this was the first day for my new business. While on the bus I was able to give away three bags of "tick-tacks", in my home room class I handed out another five bags, and from then until lunch I was able to distribute another seven bags. With the five bags I had left, my plan was to give three of them to a group of guys from the basketball team, which I considered guaranteed future customers. As I gave out each bag, I remembered what Big O told me to say. I told each person, "Don't step up unless you're ready to stand up!" I assured everyone that I would have more bags on Monday and that the cost was $5 dollars per bag.

As I was walking past the football field, a huge man-like boy approached me. I assumed he was a member of the football team because I had never seen someone that large in school before.

"What up with the free bags you've been handing out?" the boy-monster asked.

Although I was quite nervous, I responded by letting him know that the bags were samples and that on Monday I would have more bags that he could purchase. Also, I informed him of Big O's saying, "Don't step up unless you're ready to stand up!"

"I can definitely stand up, so give me all the free bags you have left!" the boy-monster demanded.

"All I have left?" I questioned. "It doesn't work like that." I responded with a little attitude. Before I could get another word out, the mountain of a boy punched me in the chest. To be honest, I never saw it coming. Also, I've never been hit like that before. I literally fell backwards and landed on the ground.

"Like I said, give me all the free bags you have left!" he repeated.

Although my fear towards this man-boy was high, I had a greater fear towards Big O and the West DA Boys. I remembered what Big O told me about what would happen to my family if I brought problems to him or his gang. All of a sudden I felt like Popeye after eating his spinach. I jumped up and said angrily, "It doesn't work like that! Here's one bag and if you want anymore, you'll need to pay for it just like everyone else." Then I finished by saying, "if you have a problem with how things are done, how about I express your dislike to Big O?" As soon as I mentioned Big O's name, the man-child took the bag and walked away. A sigh of relief hung over me like a cheap suit. I couldn't believe what had just happened, yet I chalked it up to an experience for becoming "The Man."

When I met with Big O the next day, he complimented me on my toughness in dealing with that huge man-child. Of course I responded positively by telling him it was all about being in business with him and the West DA Boys. My most overwhelming concern was how he knew about the boy-monster situation.

Big O's response was, "anything that deals with my money is watched with eagle eyes." He also assured me that a message would be delivered to the man-beast in such a way, that he won't be an issue again. Although I was grateful for whatever Big O had in stored for that jerk, I was more appreciative of his compliment about my toughness. He expressed to me that my actions ensured him that he could trust me.

Before leaving Big O's meeting place, I expressed my desire to be his top producer with the "tick-tacks." I then placed the twenty new bags into my book bag and headed out. While walking back home, I felt untouchable. I knew I would be a target for more situations like I had with that man-boy at school, yet I also knew Big O was watching and had my back. It was like I had my own personal body guard; therefore, I had nothing to worry about.

When I arrived at school on Monday morning, some of my free bag customers where already waiting to give me money for so more "tick-tacks." Business was so good that I had twelve bags sold before the end of homeroom period. By the time lunch was over, all twenty of my bags had been sold. I quickly texted Big O and told him that I needed more bags. People were coming from every direction asking me for "tick-tacks." I was becoming so popular, that I too started to become curious about the effects of this new product. That feeling didn't last very long because I didn't have any desires of using drugs. I just wanted to make as much money as possible.

As school was letting out, I received a text telling me to meet behind the bleachers at the football field. It was from Big O and I knew he was excited to hear that I completely sold all of my bags in only half a day. His quick response to refill my stash was a sign of his gratitude towards my efforts.

As I approached the field, I recognized members of the West DA Boys keeping an eye out. Not knowing the proper protocol I nodded at each of them as I passed. The strange thing was, not one of the guys nodded or said anything back to me. When I reached Big O, he explained to me that the crew was there to ensure that nothing negative was going to happen during our exchange.

"You've done a great job!" Big O expressed as he handed me a small sports bag.

"Thank you," I responded as simultaneously I handed him his money, which was $180 dollars. After the exchange, I asked why the guys would not speak to me as I passed.

Big O looked at me and simple responded by saying, "You may work with us, but you're not one of us! However, if you keep doing what you're doing, that could change quickly."

I knew exactly what Big O was saying. Although we were partners, we weren't family. I'm sure everyone with the West DA Boys had to go through some type of entrance acceptance; therefore, maybe this one was mine.

As I left our little meeting, Big O reached out to shake my hand and he said, "If you keep doing what you did today, you'll be my top producer by far. Go out there and make me proud little man."

Since our meeting went a little longer than expected, I was running late for the bus. As moving as Big O's words were, it was not enough to make me want to walk home. I quickly ran to where the bus pick-up was. Lucky for me there was a lot of traffic that day. Even though the bus had pulled away from its spot, the driver still let me on. On the trip home I was able to get rid of four more bags very easily; however, it was the next sale that was a bit of a shock.

As we arrived at my stop and got off the bus, some friends and I were heading home when a car rolled slowly towards us.

"Who's that?" one of my friends asked.

Just then the passenger side window went down. It was that big beast-boy I had a situation with earlier. I nearly lost my bowels on myself.

"I need two bags," the mountain of boy said as he leaned out of the window of the car.

I slowly approached the car and responded, "Excuse me?" Although I said it with a little attitude, trust me, I was shaking in my tennis shoes. Before the man-beast could respond, I turned toward my friends and told them to go on without me. I didn't want to conduct business in front of them.

"Give me two bags," he repeated. As he stuck his arm out the window, he slowly opened his fist and handed me the full payment for both bags. I was shocked by his change in behavior, but then it dawned on me, Big O did say that the West DA Boys had a conversation with him. Although I was still a little nervous, I made sure to get the money first before I gave the man-boy his two bags.

"Cool deal," he said as he and his friend drove off.

Whatever Big O and the West DA Boys said to that guy, it worked. As I continued to walk home, I couldn't stop thinking about the powerful feeling I had, thanks to the West DA Boys having my back. The respect I was earning was a sign that I was well on my way to becoming "The Man."

CHAPTER 7

EXPANSION

A long with the "tick-tack" business, I was still selling candy and exams. Although it was not a lot candy, I could not give up my first creation. When it came to exams, I was able to get some from five different teachers. Four of the five teachers were actually mines; there was Mr. Lopez in Civics, Mrs. Jones in Science, Mrs. Gonzalez in world history, Mr. Abbott in math, and Ms. Nunez in physics. Although this was a new school, I still kept the same speech for all my customers. My main focus was that they didn't get every question correct because it would throw up red flags. Of course I also didn't want them to talk about where they got the exam answers, if they ever got caught.

As for my new endeavor, I was doing an average of sixty bags a week. Although my money intake wasn't as great as I wanted it to be, my growth in popularity and power made up the difference. With all of my business involvements added together, I was earning over $1200 dollars a month. The amount of cash I had was so plentiful, that I had to create another hiding place to hold it all. I had seen many stories on television about people putting money in their mattress or digging a hole in the backyard and putting it there, but I chose something different. I cut a hole in the wall of my room behind the head board of my bed. I then put a false cover over it to look like the wall had never been touched. I was able to fit a lock box inside the hole, which is where I hid my money.

Business was going so well, that I needed to take advantage of the good that was happening. More opportunity also meant more risk, but I was willing to go for it. My ideal was to bring in some extra help; however, I had to decide which business the assistance would be a part of. Do I use the help to get additional teacher's exams or do I use the help to expand my customer base in selling the exams? Do I use the help with getting more candy or actually selling the candy? Lastly, do I use the help with Big O's "tick-tack" business, which of course would have to be cleared first by Big O and the West DA Boys?

In thinking back to some of my favorite movies, it's obvious that the only way to expand and grow a business, one must duplicate themselves. In other words, a person must put their trust in someone else. That means a person must be willing to reveal secrets that have made them successful in order to provide the opportunity of success for that other person. That process becomes tough because the other issue that bothered me was whether the help I developed decides to be loyal to me or take my ideas to benefit themselves. I guess that's where the trust comes in, but as you see, it makes my decision a lot more difficult.

After pondering my dilemma for a few days, it finally hit me. I should start my expansion by using friends to help with my personal business. I'll choose friends from other classes, that way I could get more exams from various other teachers and get an entirely different customer base. I would need to scout the actions of these other teachers, but it would be worth it because the money would more than make up for the work I needed to put in. This would also open the door for more opportunities to meet new people for my partnership business with Big O and the West DA Boys.

I spoke with a couple of friends I played basketball with at the park. I choose those guys because they already had knowledge of what I was doing, both on my own and with Big O and the West DA Boys. When they heard of the opportunity to participate in my exam business, of course they jumped at the chance to be called employees. I chose for them to be involved with my exam business because without permission from Big O and the West DA Boys, my friends couldn't do anything to help me in the "tick-tack" business. Their only responsibility was setting up new clients and teachers. Once I got those guys set up, I was able to speak to three other friends and get their buy in as well.

Having a team of five people would allow me time that is more devoted to my "tick-tack" business and achieving the goal I expressed to Big O. I wanted to become his highest selling agent. As hard as it's going to be, I needed to put my trust in others in order to reach the levels of success I desired.

I decided to pay my guys $1 dollar for each exam they were responsible for selling. Although, I would physically have the exam answers with me, the clients that my guys set up would count towards their income. When the new journey began, although it was difficult, business was amazing! I had customers coming from every direction. The money was great and my team was working like a well-oiled machine. Having five new team members allowed my exam business to increase nearly 300%. Although I was giving up $1 for each exam sold, my income was greatly on the rise.

With the extra help in my exam business, I was able to focus more quality time on the "tick-tack" partnership with Big O and the West DA Boys. I had so many customers that the twenty bags that Big O was giving me increased to forty at a time. It was okay for me to have that much merchandise because the West DA Boys were always around watching my back. Just like with my exam business, my partnership endeavor in the "tick-tack" business was going strong. I was selling almost 125 bags a week consistently. Some weeks I made it to 200 bags, but that was usually due to some long weekends, which meant we had a day off from school. Business was going well in every way possible.

There's an old saying that states, "What goes up, must come down." When it comes to any involvement, a person has to be prepared for such a situation. One day I experienced the downside of business production. While making my way out of a teacher's classroom, as I opened the door, the teacher was trying to put her key in, to enter the same class.

"What are you doing in my classroom?" the teacher asked.

I was so shocked, that I could not respond. I thought about running, but that would really make me look guilty. My reaction reminded me of when I first got into my candy business. I thought I was over letting fear control me like that, but I guess I was wrong.

As I stood there frozen, the teacher repeated again, "I asked you a question, what are you doing in my classroom?"

The only thing I could do was come up with a lie, but it had to be a convincing one. I looked up at the teacher and responded, "I was looking for my notebook, which I left in my teacher's class next door. Since his room was locked, I went around to the connecting rooms and just my luck, yours was open." I figured this was a good enough excuse to help get me out of the trouble I was in.

"My door wasn't unlocked," the teacher responded. "I personally locked it when I left for the cafeteria."

You would think that with a response like that, I was caught, but I held true to my lie. "I don't know about that, but as I checked the other doors they wouldn't open; however, when I checked yours, it was unlocked," I said again.

The teacher walked into the room and as she looked around to see if anything was missing she asked if I was able to get my notebook. Of course I responded by saying no, since I did not have a notebook in my hands to make my story convincing. The teacher then asked me for my name. After answering her questions, she finally told me to head back to the lunch area and to check with the teacher later to get my notebook back. I showed respect by saying I understood and apologized as I walked away. Due to the scary situation I just faced, I thought it would probably be best if I had a lookout in the future. That way I could be aware of any surprises before they happened.

As I returned to the lunchroom, I met with my friend who was the contact for the teacher I just had the situation with. Although we were able to laugh about it, the outcome could have been a lot worse. The good thing was that I did get a picture of a few exams that the teacher was going to give in the next couple of weeks. With all the excitement that occurred, I was still able to focus on business and achieve the success I wanted. That was actually a lesson I passed over to the guys who worked with me.

The business I was involved in was not an exact science; therefore, I and we would face a great deal of trial and error. This situation was one of those opportunities where I was forced to learn and overcome an obstacle. My quick thinking was a true sign of the reality of me becoming "The Man!"

CHAPTER

8

UNCOVERED SECRET

fter about two more years of great success with my candy, my exam and the "tick-tack" business with Big O and the West DA Boys, I finally hit another obstacle. I was making so much money, due to the assistance of my friends, which helped to expand my business opportunities. My income, at this point, was well over $2,500 dollars a month. The problem I was experiencing was my ability to hide those earnings. The first time I faced this problem, I put money in the leg of my bed. The second time, I cut a hole in my wall and then hid the money in a lock box within that wall. Now my problem has gotten a lot greater. The money I have been making is at a level that people with real 9 to 5 jobs face. Those people usually put their money in a bank, yet I could not do that because it would create a record of my earnings. Those earnings would be something I couldn't explain to my mother or anyone else who would inquire.

I decided to go out and purchased a small safe that I was able to hide on a top shelf in our garage. My father built that shelf to hold our Christmas decorations, along with other storage items. My mother has never gone up there. Anytime she needed something from that shelf, either my brother or I would climb up there and get it. I waited for an opportunity when my mother wasn't home and I had some members of my sells team help get the safe hidden in the garage. I covered the safe up with some of the storage items already up there. I gathered almost all of the money from both my cash box in the wall and my bedpost, and then I placed it in the safe.

The reason why I did not take all the money was that if I ever needed some and my mother was home, I could still have easy access to the rewards of my hard labor. Little did I know, that decision would come back to haunt me.

A few weeks after creating the new space for my money, I received a text from my mom. I was at the park playing basketball with my friends, yet I left as soon as I read her message. The text asked me to come home as soon as possible. I did not know what was going on, but I hurried home as quickly as I could. When I arrived at the house, my mom was sitting at the kitchen table with tears in her eyes.

"What's the matter mom?" I said as I walked over to where she was sitting.

My mom stood up and with an attitude shouted, "What are you involved in?"

I didn't know exactly what she was talking about, so I stood there quietly.

"I was cleaning the house and when I got to your room, I thought it would be nice to help you out. As I started sweeping under your bed, I felt a softness in the wall. When I moved your bed, I noticed a false cover. Behind that fake doorway I found this locked box." She had the box sitting on the counter. "What are you hiding in my wall?"

I have been hiding my way of life for the past six plus years, now I had to give an answer. There was no avoiding the evidence my mom had found. At her request, I opened the box and she saw close to $500 dollars in it. The only reason why I felt comfortable opening the box was because I had just unloaded close to $20,000 dollars into my new safe, which was hiding in the garage. I figured it would be a lot easier to make up a story that explained having $500 dollars than it would be to explain thousands of dollars.

"Where did you get this money from?" she asked again.

My plan for such a situation was to give details about my candy selling business and not the other adventures. I knew this story would appear more innocent; therefore, be more forgivable. I told her that I had been selling candy for the past four years. I started off by taking candy until I was able to purchase a little at a time. The business became so successful, that I started hiding money away. I reminded her about how I haven't asked for any money in a long time. My excuse was that I was trying to make things easier for her, but before I could finish expressing myself, she went off.

"I don't need your help! Your responsibility is to grow up, go to school and be the best person you can possibly be," she shouted. "You have never heard me complain about needing anything from any of you kids."

I quickly jumped in and played the role of wanting to be helpful. I expressed that I knew she didn't ask for anything, but that doesn't stop me for wanting to do what I can to make things easier.

She continued to express her anger, "I don't need your help! I especially don't need you out there doing illegal things. One wrong doesn't equal any kind of right," she quoted. "Although it was only about $500 dollars, which really isn't much, that's $500 dollars of the Devil's work," she stated.

"You're right!" I responded, as I dropped my head in embarrassment. "I was only trying to help, since dad is no longer around," I mumbled to her.

I knew talking about my father would help to drop the anger my mother was expressing towards me. This would open the door for a little empathy because it showed that I was trying to fill the shoes of someone I thought a great deal about.

"Whatever it is you're trying to do, it doesn't help me," my mom said as she lowered her tone. "If you really want to help me, then live life the way your father would have wanted you to. I truly believe that this isn't a characteristic either of us desire from you. Be the God fearing young man we trained you to be."

I agreed with her, but as quickly as I was able to reduce my mom's anger, I then increased it to an even higher level. I expressed that God hasn't been looking out for us ever since he took my dad. My mom, without hesitation, jumped to her feet and put her finger right in my face.

"Don't you ever speak like that again," she said. "We may not have a lot of things, but we do have what we need. We were never promised a perfect life here, and yet we're blessed all the same," she expressed with conviction.

I knew she was right, but being the teenager I was, I kept talking trying to get her to understand my point of view. "I know we're not promised a perfect life here, but don't we have to work for the things we want or should we just sit back and wait for things to happen?" I questioned, as it appeared that the focus of our conversation had been taken off of me.

"You're right son, we do need to work for the things we want, but that doesn't mean we should do wrong things to accomplish those wants," my mom responded. "God provides us with the things we need; however, many times we mix up the things we want with the things we need."

There was nothing I could say because I knew my mom was right; however, she continued her explanations. "Although $500 dollars may not be a lot of money, when you're doing wrong things, it makes the fall you eventually take even harder. Generally, a fall from respectable means builds great character, but a fall from wrong actions could mean death."

Still, everything my mom said was absolutely correct, but my goal was to become "The Man," and doing it her way wasn't going to allow that to happen for me. I ended our conversation by apologizing, but I also reminded her that I was only trying to help.

As my mom hugged me, she said, "We'll figure out the money situation later, but that's not something you need to worry yourself about. What I need you to do is go to school and be the young man we raised you to be," she said as she starred deep into my eyes.

As I walked to my room, I continued playing the role of the embarrassed victim. The truth was, the only thought on my mind at that time was how to prevent the situation of getting caught from happening again. I needed to be very careful because I wasn't going to give up the life I had created. Don't get me wrong, I agree with what my mom said; however, success is a benefit for those who fight for it, not for those who sit back and wish.

As I sat in my room, I spent time texting my team members and stressing how we needed to be extra careful. I informed them of how my mom found some of my money and how important it was to protect everything that could lead to the reality of what we were doing. The guys needed to also understand that if they ever got caught, do what needs to be done, but don't give up any unnecessary information. Basically, don't rat me out.

It was hard for me to sleep that night because I needed to come up with another hiding place for my money. Although the safe in the garage was good, I needed to be sure that my mom wouldn't accidentally find my money again. As much as I love my mom, I love my money too and losing it due to her luckiness at uncovering my hiding place was not an option.

As I continued to struggle with my thoughts of finding a more secure hiding place, it finally came to me. This new hiding place would be a lot better than the garage. Our house has an attic and the entrance is through a ceiling door in the hallway. Once you pull the string to open the door, a stair case drops down to provide access into the attic. The attic is a place that my mom has never and will never go in because of her fear. To be honest, I've always been afraid too, but I'd learn to get over those fears for the protection of my money. Aside for the cobwebs, there was insulation, wiring, and other house crap that would make a great hiding place for my safe.

Every business has its obstacles to overcome and in my case one of those obstacles was my mother. As things occur, just like in business, one must learn from the situations and move on. This is what people define as growth. My plans are still the same. I want to gain power and money, which is a direct path to becoming, "The Man."

CHAPTER 9

BACK TO BUSINESS

From a distance, I could hear footsteps walking in my direction. This was a truthful reality of my current situation. I guess everyone eventually faces the reality of life and it's easily defined by the emotions expressed though one's body. Palms begin to sweat, your heart beat speeds up, and your body feels like a sack of potatoes. The scariest thing is that there's nothing you can do about it because what's done is done.

While my boys and I were sitting outside before school started, I reminded them of the incident with my mom and her finding my money. I stressed to them that bad things will happen; however, when they do just focus on ending the situation and keep business going. I didn't discuss the amount of money my mom found because the important thing was that she found it. Besides, if they ever knew how much I was really making, they might demand more, which would be another obstacle I would have to deal with.

As we began heading to class, I got a call from Big O. He told me that there was another adventure he wanted to pursue and I was the first person who came to mind. He instructed me to meet him after school behind the football field where we've met many times before. The fact that my name came to mind first, for Big O, was a great compliment to all that I was doing. I felt that one of two things was going to happen, either we were going to work with the same type of partnership or he was ready to initiate me as a member into the West DA Boys. Just the thought of becoming a member of the West DA Boys filled my head to such a degree that I couldn't concentrate in any of my classes for the rest of the day.

Although I was able to conduct business as usual, I couldn't wait for school to end and have my meeting with Big O. The situation with my mom was still a bother, but business was a priority; therefore, it needed to continue. I knew that whatever Big O had planned, I was going to have a great opportunity to increase both my business and my money.

When the school day finally came to an end, the excitement of meeting with Big O and possibly becoming a member of the West DA Boys consumed my every thought, just as it did earlier that morning. I knew Big O was already at the meeting spot because I passed a number of the West DA Boys who were standing around as both lookouts and protection.

As usual, none of the members said a word to me. When I finally got face to face with Big O, he began our conversation with a compliment.

"Great job out there!" he stated. "You're one of my best earners when it comes to our "tick-tack" business. In other words, I greatly appreciate your efforts."

I was honored by Big O's statement, yet all I could do was stand there and smile.

"When it comes to your work ethics and your desire to be the best, there was no way I could let this opportunity pass you up," he explained. "We're starting a new business where we import and export car stereo systems. We have head units, speakers, amplifiers, and everything else that makes the music in a car bump."

The smile of excitement slowly melted from my face. Although the meeting was about another business opportunity, I was really hoping it was going to be about an initiation into the West DA Boys. Due to my established customer base, Big O believed that I had a great insight to the needs of young people looking to repair and fix up their rides. I would be a middle man, just like the guys I had working for me. My responsibility was to question people about wanting a car stereo system, then scheduling them for the West DA Boys to complete the sale and installation. For every deal completed, I would receive $25 dollars.

After Big O finished explaining the ends and outs of this new business endeavor, he questioned me to see if I was in or not. Of course I answered yes. Although I didn't get what I wanted, I still needed to show Big O that I was deserving of any opportunity to become a West DA Boy. Once the arrangements were completed, Big O and his boys left our location. I was instructed to wait until they were gone before heading out, that way people couldn't put us together. I knew I had already missed the bus, so it was no problem waiting behind. I figured it would be best if I walked home because I had a lot of thinking to do. Being the middle man in any transaction was a far cry from being "The Man." The question I kept battling with was how I could turn this opportunity into a more positive benefit for myself.

During my walk home, I was able to sell a few "tick-tack" bags and a couple of exams. Making money was one way to help me feel better about any situation I was experiencing, just like eating. When I finally got home, I realized that my mom was already there. To my surprise, she had gotten off work early.

"Why are you home so late?" she asked.

I knew she was really wondering if I was still doing the things that inspired our last conversation. I told her that I missed the bus; therefore, I had to walk home. She looked at me with curiosity in her eyes, but I stuck to my story. As she walked over to me, she instructed that I empty my pockets and my book bag. I had no problem doing it because I kept all the merchandise in a special compartment I built in my bag. I did that for such a situation like this, but I thought a school administrator, a police officer, or someone trying to rob me would be the ones to test it. In this case, it was my mom.

Once she realized that there was nothing of interest on my person, she gave me a hug and walked away without saying another word. Even though I knew what she was doing, I just played dumb and let it go.

While sitting in my room, it dawned on me how to stay on track with becoming "The Man" with Big O's new business adventure. All I needed to do was learn how to install car stereo systems myself. Learning how to install a car stereo system would also teach me how to remove one. With those skills, the only other thing I needed to learn was how to pick car door locks.

The big question was where could I learn all those things without revealing what I was really trying to do? I couldn't go to Big O or ask any of the West DA Boys. I had no clue of where to go for this experience. All of a sudden it hit me like a shot. The best way to kill two birds with one stone was to get a part time job at a car stereo shop learning how to do installations. Having that type of job would give me the opportunity to not only learn about installations, but also help me better understand other auto mechanisms, like car alarms and door locks. This would also be a good cover from my mom for buying myself a used car.

With all the excitement of possibly working at a car stereo shop, I needed to also find a way to balance all of my other adventures. I needed to keep my exam sales going, as well as both businesses I had with Big O and the West DA Boys. I was alright with letting the candy business go. Even though all this sounds like a lot of work, to me, it was just another pathway to becoming "The Man."

I started right away trying to find a job at a car stereo shop that was willing to hire someone based on their desire to work and not on their experiences. I used every story possible to get hired. I said I needed to earn money to be able to pay for my senior prom; I needed to help my family with financial needs due to the loss of my father; and I even used the old famous just give me a chance to show what I can do. Things looked real bleak, until I arrived at my lucky number seven choice. This place was a little hole in the wall, yet they were willing to take a chance on someone like me.

I hurried home to tell my mom about the new opportunity I received. Of course she was excited and I knew that this would look like a major move forward in her eyes. Considering my mom's attitude from her discovery of my hidden money, this job would make for a good cover. Although she never said anything, I knew she was still suspicious of what I was doing. She let that show when she questioned me for coming home late from school and asked me to empty my pockets and book bag. With all that goes on in our area, my mom had every right to think whatever negative thoughts she had about my dealings; however, it was up to me to do a better job at hiding my actions from her.

Having this job forced me to take a step backwards with my other business adventures. Since I would be working after school, it would definitely get in the way of me seeing customers. In order for my business to continue at the level I had established, I would need to give product to my team members. This would give them more responsibility, which means more power. That power could also lead to more control. Based on the idea of losing some degree of power and control, I questioned whether or not to move forward with my plan of providing products.

With the thought of starting a real job and continuing the business opportunities I was already involved in, my mind was going crazy. I couldn't fall asleep that evening due to all the thoughts I had going through my head. As the night continued, it felt like I saw every minute as it passed on the clock. All I kept doing was tossing and turning in my covers. How could I give up all that I had created? This question haunted me all night long.

Around 4:30 in the morning, the answer hit me like a flash of lightning. In order for me to keep control and power within my businesses, I would only give my team products for pre-arranged appointments. Without having extra product, it forces my team to still rely on me in order to satisfy customers. Continuing to have control and power would keep me in line with achieving my goals. My efforts with Big O and the West DA Boys, along with the new adventure we created, and of course my exam business, would continue to keep me on the pathway to becoming "The Man."

CHAPTER 10

DEVELOPMENT

Work has been going great. I've learned how to install a stereo system in a car dashboard, in the trunk of a car, and under the seats as well. I've also learned how to install speakers in doors, floors, and various kits. Kits are speaker boxes that contain either one or multiple speakers and they are installed in a variety of places in a car. The electrical set up, to me, is the most difficult part of the installation. Learning about which wires go where and how to hide them throughout the vehicle is a work of genius. That of course takes a bit longer to learn than the two months I have been working in this field.

Having a legitimate job, has allowed me the opportunity to open a bank account. Having an account, has allowed me the ability to deposit some of my other earnings as well; however, I had to watch how much I put into the account. Since my mom co-signed for me, she had access to my financial activities.

As for my other business adventures, they did take a step back, yet my production level was still high. Although Big O was still a big concern, I knew he was happy with the connections I provided for him in reference to our new car stereo sales business. In the two months I had been working at installing car stereos, I referred more than a dozen contacts to Big O. I believe it's safe to say, I was still in his favor.

The one question I had in reference to Big O's car stereo business was where he was getting his products from? The cost he charged was a lot lower than what the shop I worked for was charging, even though the actual products were the same. He told me they were importing and exporting product.

Then it hit me, although the answer was starring me right in the face the whole time. His stereos were stolen. Since his products were hot, it did not matter how much or how little the cost he charged, it was all pure profit. Big O's stereo business was similar to my candy adventure. Although I was jacking them from different places, there was never a cost to me, which meant whatever price I sold them for, it was all profit. The difference between our two businesses was that his was more complex and had a higher value than mine.

With all this information swirling through my head, I eventually came up with a great plan. With the knowledge I was developing from working in the installation business, I too could benefit from establishing my own private customers. After having more time at learning the installation game and finding a way to get my hands on some merchandise, I'll be ready to keep some of the contacts for myself. With keeping only a small number of contacts, I'd more than make-up for the money I was losing from taking a real job.

Over the next four weeks, I came up with a plan for getting some merchandise. I've already compared Big O's business to my candy adventure, so why not establish things the same way I did back then. I've been watching the delivery trucks for a good while now and the routine of the driver was pretty obvious. We had a very attractive young lady working the front desk at the shop. Just like many of our customers, the driver would always stop off and flirt with her as he came to deliver products. He would be there talking to her a minimum of ten minutes every time. That was more than enough time for me to make my move and get the merchandise I needed. I would also use my employee discount to buy some of the small things I needed to properly complete an installation.

Before I could consider starting my own stereo business, I needed to secure my own transportation. I needed to get myself a car and become my own first client. I would have a system that would serve as great advertisement for my own business. This wouldn't be an issue for Big O because he would assume that my system was installed at my place of business. As good as the idea appeared, I still needed to actually find a car to buy.

To keep my mom thinking positive about me, I decided to ask for help with looking for a car. I told my mom that I had saved almost $2,500 dollars towards buying a car. Of course she was impressed and that was my goal. I also informed her that I enrolled in a driver's aid course at school, which would help me as I moved forwarded at getting my license. This made me look more responsible and showed a sense of dedication to my goals. All of these things represented great signs for my mom to assume that I was changing from the person she thought I was becoming.

After a few weeks of driver's training, I was successfully able to pass the written portion of the driver's test and secured my learners permit. This made me, as well as my mom, extremely happy. An even bigger surprise came a few weeks later, when I got home from work. My mom informed me that a friend of hers had a car for sale. It was an old Honda Civic, which is a good fixer upper car. The cool thing was that she was only charging $3,000 dollars. An even bigger surprise was that my mom paid half the cost. As excited as I was, I did feel a little guilty.

My mom continued complementing me on my efforts at developing in a positive direction. She expressed how proud of me she was since I was both working and going to school. Although I was feeling guilty inside, I could not let those emotions hinder me from achieving my goal at becoming "The Man."

Now that I had my car, it was time for me get my license and kick my new adventure into existence. I began to keep a close eye on the patterns of the delivery guy who came to our shop. His routine was still the same for each delivery. He came into the shop, spent a few minutes greeting the young lady at the front desk, unloaded the merchandise, and then he spent more time flirting with the front desk girl again. All in all, he was there for almost twenty minutes on each delivery. He parked his truck in the alley behind the store, where the employees parked. The cameras out there were only on when the store was closed. During the day, the only cameras that were active were all inside the shop.

My goal was to get a few stereos and speakers each week until I built up my supplies. Anything outside of those major components, like wires, plugs, and whatever else, I would buy from the shop using my employee discount. Although I continued to work hard, I needed to prepare to execute my plan. There's an old saying that states, "Never bite the hand that feeds you." In other words, do not act negatively towards the positive that's provided for you. Knowing all that psychological babel, I was still planning to do exactly the opposite.

After being employed for the past six months, it was time for me to put my plans into motion. My other businesses were still going well. People were buying exams like crazy. Most of the teachers that I had exams for kept using the same schedules each term, which meant they used the same tests. As students purchased the exams, I informed them that some questions may have changed, so be aware. If anyone complained about changes, I would have consider updating my materials, but that didn't happen. As for my "tick-tack" business, sales continued to operate at the highest level. With all the success I was experiencing, there was no doubt in my mind that my stereo installation business would produce the same rewards.

Shortly after I qualified for my license, the day came for me to finally execute my new business plan. I quickly positioned myself as the delivery guy arrived. My plan was to get in and out of his truck as quickly as possible. Once he finished packing his dolly and entered into the shop, I made my way to the back of his truck. I got my hands on two stereo head units and one set of speakers. With all the adrenaline running through my body, I moved a lot faster than anticipated. I was able to get everything loaded into my car and return back to the store with time to spare. The delivery guy had already unloaded his stock and was still flirting with our front desk girl. This process went on about twice a week for just under one month. That's when I got my first sale.

A guy came into the shop looking to get a new stereo system installed in his car. It was obvious that he couldn't afford the cost of what he was looking for, so I targeted him as a prospect. I spoke to him as if he was going to be a customer for Big O, but in reality he was going to be my first client. After haggling for about twenty minutes, we agreed upon a stereo system and two kits, each with one ten inch woofer and a four-inch mid-range for $875 dollars including installation. The regular price for such a system would normally cost about $1,800 dollars. Even though he interpreted this deal as a $925 dollar savings, I looked at this as 100% percent profit.

I continued this same process for the next few months. For every eight or so referrals I sent to Big O, I kept one or two. Business was moving a lot faster than I had hoped; therefore, I had to increase my product retrieval in order to keep up with the demand.

Since things were going so well with all of my other involvements, I became comfortable, which in the end generally leads to carelessness.

I had been taking product from the delivery guy for about four months and since nothing was ever expressed, I assumed all was good. Stereo equipment is a lot more expensive than candy bars; therefore, if anything turned up missing, one would think something would have been said. The one thing I didn't count on was that actions are different when involving valuables.

One Saturday morning, when I arrived at work, my boss called me into his office. I didn't know what to expect, but when I walked in, I noticed two other guys sitting there. After being instructed to take a seat, one of the other guys began showing a video recording from the inside of the delivery truck I had been taking product from.

"We had cameras installed in our trucks for the purpose of monitoring our drivers and ensuring their integrity," the one guy expressed. "As we began tracking missing equipment, this video revealed the innocents of our employee, but the guiltiness of you!" The man said as he pointed right at me.

Just then, the video showed me climbing into the back of the truck and grabbing boxes of equipment. The interesting thing about the video was that they did not stop with one; they had me on camera eight times removing product from their truck. Before I could say anything, two police officers walked into the room.

"Please stand up young man," one of the officers said. "Place your hands behind your back because you're under arrest."

As much as I wanted to give an excuse, I knew what kind of life I was getting into, so I couldn't say anything. Being arrested was just another experience I needed to go through. My biggest concern wasn't the fact that I was being arrested, it was the thought of facing my mom once she finds out. Something like this is going to hurt her tremendously, considering what we went through in our last falling out. Needless to say, as the officers where escorting me out of the office, my boss put a cherry on top of the situation.

"Just in case you haven't figured things out, YOU'RE FIRED!!!" he said angrily.

CHAPTER 11

JUVENILE

The one thing I remembered Big O always saying about getting caught, was to never give his or anyone's name. With the various contacts he had throughout the city, he'd find out where anyone was and he'd make sure things got taken care of. If I or anyone every gives names, especially his, then he'll find that out too and that person will be dealt with. Since this was the first serious situation I'd gotten myself into, I had to rely on the words of Big O. I had to play it calm and just wait for the process to run its course.

My mom; however, was another story. I knew she would be angry. To be honest, she may be so angry that she'll probably let me stay and rot in jail. The sad thing is that I'd possibly be safer in jail than I would be if I were with her. Although I never wanted to put my mom or anyone for that matter through this hassle, it's all a part of the process towards achieving my desired goal. I am sure I will get through whatever it is I have to experience and the credibility will go a long way for me. With all that going on, I was still very concerned about my mom.

As we arrived at the police station, I was escorted to a desk. There I was booked and fingerprinted. I was also informed that my car was towed and impounded, which didn't matter because I truly believe that my mom was going to take it away. Although she only paid half of the cost, she did so as a sign of respect and proudness towards me; however, with the situation I'm in now, I guess I've destroyed her views.

After the officers completed their paperwork, I was placed in a holding cell while they contacted my mom. Since I was still considered a minor, they had to contact a guardian on my behalf. I could only imagine how that conversation would go.

The reality of where I was started kicking in, yet I could not let myself become emotional. First impressions are very big when in jail; therefore, crying defines someone as being soft and that's not a good way to begin this process. There were about a dozen other guys in the holding cell with me; however, everyone was sitting around minding their own business. While waiting, I realized that a couple of hours had passed and I had not heard anything in reference to my mom or Big O. I asked the attending officer whether my mom or anyone had been contacted. He had no answer in regards to my situation; however, he did assure me that he would look into it and get back to me.

While heading back to my seat, one of the other guys approached me and asked what set I was claiming? Not wanting to get into a conversation with him, I responded by saying I was good. I guess that was the wrong answer because he stood in my way as I tried to go around him.

"I asked what set you're claiming," he repeated in an aggressive voice.

By this time we had the attention of the other guys in the cell. I didn't know how to answer the guy's questions because I really wasn't affiliated with any set. Since I wasn't an official West DA member, I figured I couldn't respond by claiming to be one. As I turned to walk away, I repeated to him, "I'm good."

This time I knew it was the wrong answer because the guy hit me in the back of the head. He hit me so hard that I flew forward onto two other guys. Needless to say, those guys weren't too happy about me landing on them. They tossed me aside as if I were a rag doll. Before matters could get worse, the guards came in to put an end to things before they could truly get bad. Although I was the only person who suffered from this little scuffle, I had to remain tough.

After about another hour in the holding cell, the attending guard called my name. My mom had arrived. I was escorted to another room where I could sit and talk with her. I knew this wasn't going to be a good conversation, but I had to accept the consequences of my actions.

"Are you alright?" she asked.

Of course, I responded by saying yes, there was no other answer for me to give.

"You just couldn't stay away from the mess you've been doing?" she said as her anger started to take over. "We talked about this pathway you were traveling down and you assured me that you were going to change. You were going to strive to be that son I could be proud of, yet look where all your lies has led us."

It was best for me to remain quiet because there was nothing I could say that would change the situation we were experiencing. The police officer had already informed my mom on what I was arrested for. He explained how they had me on video taking stereo equipment, multiple times, from the back of a delivery truck.

"You've pushed me to my limit," my mom said as she continued to fuss. "I'm going to do whatever I can to help you through this situation, but after that you're on your own!"

I could tell she meant what she was saying and I could not blame her. This experience was a process I needed to face, in order to achieve the goal I was ultimately shooting for. With all that being said, as angry as I knew she was, I still wasn't ready to hear her ranting and raving about me not doing the right thing.

"I love you, but I can't have you in my house anymore" my mom said. "I'm going to let you stay here as long as the courts see fit. You need to experience the consequences of your actions," she explained. "You'll need to show a great deal of growth and change in order to regain my confidence in you," she expressed as she got up and walked towards the door.

I knew this was tough for her and believe it or not, it was tough for me too. Although this was something I needed to have in order to gain street credit, it was very difficult. I guess it's like getting a shot from the doctor. You know it's coming, but you really don't want it, even though it's necessary. It was shocking to hear those words come out of my mom's mouth because no child wants or thinks they can lose the support of their parent. A mother's love is always expected. It was hard for me to hold back my tears, but I had to remember where I was. The officer let me sit there for a few minutes while I regained my composure and then he took me back into the holding cell.

While walking back to the cell an emergency alarm sounded. Two inmates had jumped someone in the cell I was in and beat him as if he had stolen something. The guy who got beat was lying unconscious in a pool of his own blood. Immediately, I wondered if all this was worth it: being in jail, living a different life in the presence of others, sneaking around, hiding money, and having to be on the defense to protect myself. As stated earlier, although this seems tough, it's needed in order to gain credibility at becoming "The Man".

As the doors closed behind me and the guards took the unconscious boy out, a familiar voice approached and said to me, "now we can finish what we started earlier." The reason why it was familiar was because it was the same guy that approached me earlier when I first got into the holding cell. "I believe you were about to tell me the set you were claiming," he said.

The first thought that entered my mind was about the guy that was beaten unconsciously. Was he too, a victim of this brute? I did not know if this person caused the other inmate's injuries, but I was not going to give him the chance to do the same to me. If I attack first, then at least I'll have a chance, while the officers come in to break us up. By standing up and fighting, I'll also show the other guys that I'm willing to defend myself.

Without giving it another I thought, I took a swing at the annoying brute; however, things didn't work out the way I had planned them. The guy must have known I would take a punch at him because he was waiting for it. He blocked my attempt and countered with a solid blow to my stomach. The punch dropped me immediately, but I jumped back up and positioned myself for a fight. Then something unexpected occurred. Two other guys stood in between the brute and myself as a protective shield. Just then, another voice spoke out, "this kid is a friend of Big O and the West DA Boys. If anyone has a problem with him, then you have a problem with us."

That simple statement made everyone back away. I guess Big O was telling the truth when he said that he'd find any of his people if they were caught. The person that spoke up on my behalf informed me that Big O wanted to make sure I was tough enough to keep my mouth shut. He also wanted to know if I had enough courage to stand my ground and fight. I guess both of those questions were answered. People will always take chances and go after you, but knowing that you'll fight back would hinder much of those opportunities. Maybe if my father had that kind of reputation he would be alive today. The question I had earlier on whether or not all of this was worth going through to becoming "The Man," was more than answered.

CHAPTER 12

THE VERDICT

The day finally came for me to stand in front of a judge. Although a guilty verdict would not be a major shock, I still hoped that there was a chance I'd be freed. Seeing the video greatly decreased much of that hope. I only saw a portion of the video and it appeared to be all the evidence needed against me. My only chance of getting out was through Big O and his connections. Lucky for me, I noticed him and a couple of other West DA members sitting in the back of the courtroom.

The officer ordered me to stand up and go in front of the judge. Talk about your butterflies, my stomach was going crazy. Even though I had a strong feeling of what the outcome would be, it was still a scary situation. My nerves were racing, my palms became sweaty, and my throat felt swollen. My heart was beating like I had just ran a marathon, but with all that going on, I had to remain as cool as possible. In this situation, it was all about appearances because if I had broken down, then everyone in jail would know.

Without much hesitation, the judge said, "I've read the accusations and I've viewed the video, which was submitted as evidence. Taking all that into consideration, I find the accused guilty as charged."

As the negative words painted a degrading picture of who I was, my body felt like a wet noodle. I had to hold onto a chair in order to refrain from falling.

As the judge kept speaking, things appeared to be moving in slow motion. "You are hereby reprimanded to spend the next eighteen months in a juvenile detention facility."

With that being said, my legs became steel rods stuck in cement. Now I was unable to move, yet to top things off, out of the corner of my eyes I saw my mom with her head buried in her hands. As bad as I felt for her, I needed to remain strong and not get emotional. Although things were tough, I knew this would eventually lead to what I was trying to accomplish.

When the judge finally concluded with his reading of the verdict, he slammed the gavel down and instructed the officers to take me away. As we walked passed my mom, she whispered to me, "I love you and I'm praying for your safety; however, you earned this."

Big O and the guys that were with him, had already left the courtroom. I assumed that they had headed back to inform everyone on what had happened. I knew it was only a matter of time before I would hear from them again.

While sitting in the holding cell waiting for the day's cases to end, I kept focus on what my ultimate goal was. Although I felt bad for what I was putting my mom through, I knew the future was going to be great because of what I was trying to accomplish. When that time comes, I know she will be appreciative of my provisions.

As we boarded the bus heading to the juvenile facility, I noticed there was about eight other inmates heading there with me. I started to get a little worried because as I scanned the group that was on the bus, I did not see the guys that saved me from the brute in the holding cell. One inmate was drawing a lot of attention to himself because he was crying uncontrollably. The guards tried to calm him down, but it was to no effect.

When we pulled up to the facility, an officer jumped onto the bus and gave us a breakdown of the center. This particular facility believed in manual labor or what some would call military discipline. Boys were digging holes, painting walls, landscaping, and doing all sorts of physical work. I immediately felt the reality of my situation once again. My heart started pumping faster and I began sweating from every part of my body.

When the guard finished talking he shouted, "Everybody off the bus!"

Once again, I knew something was wrong because my body wouldn't move. Although I've faced a great deal of emotional drama these past few hours, nothing felt like it did when I was instructed to get off the bus. I was not alone with my physical boundaries because some of the other guys could not move either.

The guard recognized what was going on so he spoke out again, "I would suggest that you all appear tough. You have earned the right to be here and any sign of weakness will make you a target for others to take advantage of you. If you were man enough to do the crime, then you have to be man enough to serve your time."

Just before reopening the bus doors, the guard expressed one last thing. "I can't promise you that everything is going to be perfect, this is a detention center; therefore, things will happen. I will suggest that you all stay on your toes and good luck to you as you serve your sentences."

After those so-called words of wisdom, we were led into the juvenile center. Each of us went through the registration process. We were stripped of our clothes and personal things, then given a common uniform. Once that portion of the process was completed we all attended an orientation where we were lectured on scheduling and obedience. We were made clear of the rules, as well as what happens to those who break those rules. The one common thought the facility wanted to teach is that life has choices. Based on the choices one makes, consequences are paid; therefore, it's up to each individual to consider the outcome before making a choice.

Once the orientation process was completed, we were then led to our living quarters. The quarters consisted of a common area bathroom, which was shared with five other rooms. Each room had two bunk beds for four guys. Aside from the basic needs, everything else was a benefit provided by those in charge. Television was a reward and those in charge decided when that right was granted. All juvenile facilities were different; however, they all pretty much were attempting to accomplish the same thing. They wanted to teach the importance of making the right choices in life.

The first few days were somewhat difficult, everyone was trying to test the new guys. Sometimes the other juveniles would walk up to one of us and say bad things, trying to get some kind of reaction. They would mess with us in the restrooms, take food from our plates, and even destroy things we had in our possession. I learned the hard way; you stand up for yourself or you keep dealing with negative actions towards you.

At first, I let many things go, but one day I got jumped while heading to the showers. It was at that point I remembered what the guard said before we unloaded off the bus, that they are not able to watch everything, so we must learn how to defend ourselves. Guys that had been at the facility for some time, knew exactly when and where they could get away with certain actions. Although I fought back, I still took some good beatings.

It was tradition; therefore common, for new inmates to show up with bruises, cuts, or some sort of physical damage on a weekly bases. Some inmates received this on a daily bases, but that was usually if they never learned to fight back. I guess this was part of the consequences for being arrested and sent to such a facility. Although fighting back did not guarantee that nothing would ever happen to you, it did reduce the occurrences.

Every week our character building responsibilities changed. As discussed earlier, this facility believed highly in physical labor as discipline for correcting one's behavior. The most difficult and dirtiest jobs always went to the new inmates and the rule breakers.

Such responsibilities were digging holes, spreading manure to fertilize the landscape,

and cleaning the sanitation tanks. You would think that after doing those jobs, no one

would ever go back to doing the things they did to earn the right to experience such work;

however, juveniles will be juveniles.

The leaders constantly repeated to us, "Until a person changes his or her thought

process, they'll never change their feelings, which influences their actions." In other words,

the way a person thinks, dictates how they feel, which dictates how they act. Everything

boils down to one's thought process.

The longest stretch of time that anyone serves at this facility is about twenty-four to

thirty-six months. My stretch was scheduled for eighteen months. After about ten months,

I was already considered a veteran. You would think that because of my time spent, it

would eliminate the negative actions one faced; however, that was not the case. I didn't

go through as much crap as a new person, but I still had to prove myself on a continuous

bases.

It was right around sixteen months of service, when two guys arrived at our facility

representing a rival gang to the West DA Boys. They made their affiliation clear from day

one. Although I was not an official member of the West DA Boys, word got around about

my relationship with them and Big O.

One day, while in the restroom, I heard the two new boys enter. I believe they came in with the intentions to do harm to me. They started talking bad about the West DA Boys and anyone who was associated with them. I knew they were only trying to get me angry, hoping that I would react physically. When I came out of the stall, I just ignored them. As they continued getting in my face and trying to annoy me, I kept thinking about only having two months left to serve, which made it easier to refrain from acting out. Although I was able to hold back, the two guys weren't. They eventually attacked me as I was walking away. I got a few good licks in, but it's safe to say that they put a good beating on me. Luckily, the guards came in to break everything up before they practically killed me.

I did not face as bad a disciplinary job as the two other inmates, yet I did inherit some new scars and bruises. My nose and lip were busted and traces of blood was all over the bathroom floor. Thanks to the guards, the report stated that I was defending myself and the other guys initiated the physical altercation. I got landscaping duties, while the other two inmates got manure responsibilities. They were also separated from one another forcing them to stand on their own. In such an environment, there are strengths in numbers. By separating the two guys, they were forced to stand alone, which in returned decreased their desire to act out and break rules.

As my time was coming to an end, I had gone through a lot. People sometimes say serving time in a juvenile facility is like being on a vacation. I can assure you, that my time was no vacation. I was more than ready to leave, as my time served was ending.

My goal of course was never to come back to such a facility; however, I did not have any plans on changing my life structure. In order to continue to achieve my ultimate desire, I needed to be more careful in my dealings. With the fine-tuning of my actions and more awareness of what's going on around me, my efforts would increase the reality of me becoming "The Man."

CHAPTER 13

AFTER THE SYSTEM

"See you on the other side," was the last thing I said as the guards escorted me out of the juvenile facility. As I said, I was more than ready to leave the center, with the goal of never returning. My time there was no vacation, but it taught me a lot. As I completed the necessary release paperwork, once again, my mom was right there. With all that I had put her through, she was still right there for me. As I approached her, a tear ran down her face.

"Thank God you're finally out!" she said emotionally. "I never stopped praying for you."

She gave me the biggest hug as she continued her flow of emotional happiness. It felt good seeing her and knowing she still had my back, even though she didn't understand why I did the things I had done.

"Let's get you out of here because I'm sure you must be hungry for some good old fashion soul food," mom said as we walked to the car.

We headed to one of my favorite restaurants, which was only a couple of blocks away from our house. When we got there, I was able to order some fried chicken, mac and cheese, collard greens, candied yams and corn bread. The excitement of getting ready to eat some real food, outside of the mess we got in the juvenile facility, showed all over my face. My mouth was dripping with saliva.

While we waited for the food to cook and be delivered, my mom started to ask me questions about my stay at the center. I expressed to her that things were tough, but I handled it. She began asking questions about the behavior of the other juveniles and the conduct of the guards. I explained to her that fighting back worked out on some occasions and at other times, it didn't go so well. There really wasn't too much trouble from the guards, at least nothing worth talking about. I know my mom was concerned about my well-being, both physically and mentally. That's why she asked so many questions. I assured her that all was good and that I am done with that part of my life. She even asked if I had been raped. At that point, I was sure it became obvious that I was becoming annoyed with all the questions; however, that did not stop my mom.

"I am only asking these questions because I need to evaluate your status on where you've been, how you are, and where you're going," she expressed while trying to eliminate my annoyance towards her questions.

Since I was only trying to say what I thought my mom wanted to hear, it made the conversation much more difficult. My goal was to try to show that I was sorry, that I got a taste of reality and that I was going to change. I wanted her to believe that I was never going to be in that situation again. It was obvious that every time I spoke, she looked deep into my soul. I felt a little uncomfortable because I knew it was all a lie. Doing things her way, would not allow me the opportunity to achieve the goal I was fighting for.

I was so happy when the server came with our food because I knew the conversation would finally end. After my mom said a prayer, we dug in and started eating. Everything was just as I had remembered. The chicken was crispy with a little spice in its seasoning, the mac and cheese was thick and creamy, and the greens had an amazing garlic taste. The yams and corn bread were satisfyingly perfect as well. I don't think it was the food that had changed, it was just me being away for so long that made it tastes so heavenly.

After dinner, there was just enough room for some sweet potato pie and banana pudding. The only way to describe how I felt after eating all that I had was that the food was out of this world. The combination of me being away for so long and my love for soul food, made this encounter a perfect experience. All I could think about was how much I missed eating like this; however, that mood was quickly changed. As I was finishing my dessert, my mom started up with the questions again.

"Now that you've missed a year and a half of school, what are your plans for graduating?" she asked.

To be honest, I hadn't thought about graduating, but I couldn't tell her that. Besides, I knew that wasn't the answer she was looking for. My response to her was that I needed to look at my options and then go from there.

"How about the changes you need to make moving forward?" she continued. "Considering our last falling out when I found all that money in your room, it looks like nothing has changed. I thought you were ready then, yet look what happened."

She was like a machine because she wouldn't stop digging into me.

"You've lost a year and a half of your life doing the things your dad and I trained you not to do and being someone we raised you not to be. Since living your way hasn't worked out, what's your plan now?" she continued to ask.

I didn't know if she really wanted an answer because she kept asking one questions after another. As the waitress came with the check, it was a much needed break. The uncomfortable silence we were having really made it hard for me. The fact that I could not give answers to her questions helped with the difficulties as well. I knew what I wanted, but I couldn't express it to my mom because that's not how she and dad raised me. As I sat there saying nothing, my mom just shook her head in disappointment. She went on to pay the bill and we gathered our things to head home.

When we got into the car, my mom made one last statement, "Just as I feared, you have no plans on moving forward in the direction you've been raised. That only leaves one pathway for you and that's the pathway that led you to being locked up for the last year and a half of your life."

As rough as it sounded, she was right. I was going to do exactly what I wanted to, in order to achieve the goals I desired. Since there was no fooling her, I just sat there quietly with my head hung down.

"Just as I feared!" she said again. The rest of the ride was done in complete silence.

When we arrived at the house, I noticed my brother and sisters were there. They each greeted me with sincere emotions and a hug. It may seem normal, but I took it to mean something was about to happen. As we all sat down to talk, my mom disappeared into her room. Although my brother and sisters wrote me every now and then, we really haven't seen much of each other for a good while. With that sibling separation, this made for a good time to reunite. Even though my attention appeared to be with them, I was really concerned about what my mom was thinking and doing while in her room.

As the afternoon turned into evening, my mom finally came out from her room. She called all of us back into the living room area. As we sat down, she began to pray. She mentioned all of us in her prayer; however, the main focus was on me. It was easy to hear the disappointment in her voice, but she also showed a lot of love and care for my future. Once she finished her prayer, she looked at me and asked the same question, "What now?"

Again, I knew what she wanted to hear, but I didn't know how to make it believable. I didn't know how to respond with the conviction I knew she was looking for. It's a lot easier to fool other people, but parents tend to know their kids better; therefore, that task becomes a little harder. After a brief moment of silence, I responded by telling her that I only wanted to make her happy. I said I was willing to do whatever she wanted me to. I felt that was a good answer. I even put on a sad face to show how sorry I was for causing her so much pain. I must admit, I thought my performance was an act of genius, considering the reactions from my brother and sisters.

My mom starred at me for what appeared to be the longest ten seconds ever. "Fool me once, shame on you, but fool me twice, shame on me," she finally expressed.

I really did not understand what she meant, but based on her tone of voice, I knew not to interrupt. I figured a long speech was going to occur, so I just sat there because it appeared that she was going to say the same things she's been saying for a while. My role was just to sit there and act like I cared.

"When I busted you last time with all that money, you claimed that you were sorry and you were going to do better; however, you kept doing the same crap," she said angrily. "You got caught and had to spend almost two years in a juvenile facility, yet when asked what your plans are for moving forward, you have no answer."

I guess I was correct. My mom was doing what most parents do, so I just let her continue because she needed to get some things off her chest.

"Serving all that time, one would think that maybe you put some deep thought into what you've done and where you're going," she stated. "The way you think, dictates how you feel, which dictates how you act," mom said as she stood up from her seat. "Your mind frame hasn't changed a bit and that's why you don't have answers for my questions. I'm sure you believe that whatever it is you're doing will create something big and powerful, but what you fail to recognize is that all you're creating is a big mess!"

Although I think my mom is smart, I guarantee she had no idea of how close she was to expressing what I was doing. She may not have understood my actions, but I think she had some idea of the outcome I was seeking. I was trying to create a bigger and better life for not only myself, but for my entire family.

As my mom walked towards me, she had tears in her eyes again. She sat next to me and grabbed my hand. In a million years, I would have never guessed what was going to happen next. As she looked deep into my eyes, one of the most difficult phrases came from her mouth.

"Baby, I love you with all my mind, heart, and soul; however, I refuse to support or condone whatever it is you're doing." Those tears that were filling her eyes, were now running down her face. "Today is Saturday, but by Monday morning you need to be out of my house. The only love you need right now, is tough love."

After saying those extremely difficult words, my mom went back into her room. My brother and sisters appeared to be just as stunned as I was to hear what our mom had just said. We all sat there in silence for quite a while. After about ten minutes, without saying a word, one by one each of them got up from their seat and left the room. I continued to sit there, still shocked about what had just happened. I realized that at that moment, for the first time, I was all alone. With all the crazy things I had been doing, my mom was always there for me, but her actions showed that even parents have a limit.

As I continued to sit there, I began to wonder if all that I was going through really worth fighting for, just to become "The Man."

CHAPTER **14**

THE MAN EMERGES

I n order to achieve the goal I wanted, such experiences like the one I was facing and what I had dealt with had to occur. As hard as it was to deal with my mom kicking me out, it had to happen eventually. The difficulty in fighting for a goal is when reality actually occurs, because nobody is prepared for it.

Now that everyone, meaning my family, has lost faith and confidence in me, I needed to use their negativity as motivation to prove them all wrong. That night I cleaned out all the money that was in my safe and I bagged up a few personal items. I then left early the next morning, before everyone woke up and headed out to church.

Due to the current situation I was in, my choices were extremely slim in reference to where I could go. I could not go to the homes of any family members, my friends, or the church members. The guys that worked with me still lived with their parents, so that wasn't an option either. With all those boundaries, only one name represented the best answer. That name was Big O.

When I arrived at the hang out where Big O and the West DA Boys stayed, everyone welcomed me. They made jokes about me having my cherry popped, which basically means being locked up for the first time. It felt strange having the guys joke around with me because they had never done that before. Usually they were serious or just ignored me all together. I desperately wanted Big O to appear because it was somewhat uncomfortable having the guys act that way towards me.

After about twenty minutes, silence spread across the room. Big O had made his appearance from one of the back rooms, along with some of the top officers in the gang. Big O walked over to where I was and stood face to face with me. As he placed his arm around my shoulders, he began to express what I had done in reference to the businesses of the West DA Boys.

"This scrub helped initiate the greatest sales history of anyone in reference to our "tick-tack" business. Week in and week out, he was our top sells person," he went on to say.

That statement alone instigated cheers from the West DA Boys, which was a great sign of respect. I was still unclear of what was happening; however, I did begin to feel more at ease.

"This scrub used his personal connections to open up additional business for us, as we advanced into our car stereo system endeavor," Big O continued with his expressions of my accomplishments. "After almost a few years of success, this scrub was labelled a delinquent juvenile. His cherry was popped, he was arrested, he was jumped multiple times as he served eighteen months in a juvenile facility and not once did he ever say anything about his new family."

Just then I realized what was happening. After all the time and effort I put into gaining the respect of the West DA Boys, I was finally accepted.

Big O turned towards me and said, "You've more than proven yourself to be a West DA Boy and after two more stages, your membership will be official."

After Big O's final words, I was attacked. I couldn't even say how many guys jumped me, but it was another opportunity for me to show my toughness. I fought as hard as I could, yet no one individual could win that battle. This task went on for approximately one minute, so they say. Forget what you see in movies and on television. I took the worst beating I had ever experienced. I was punched, kicked, tackled, and thrown around like a rag doll, yet with all that, I still got a few good licks in.

Eventually, the attack came to an end as a voice cried out, "That's enough!"

With all the blood and pain I was dealing with, I remained focused on the end-result, which of course helped me get over the physical struggles I was facing.

"Let's get him ready for his family markings," Big O stated.

I was burned in three places; on my right arm I received a sword of honor, on the center of my back I received two eyes symbolizing the family looking out for me, and on my left chest I received a shield of protection. Although they were small markings, if you thought the beating was painful, this was worst. Once completed, I was greeted as a new member of the West DA Boys.

Every member of the West DA Boys served a purpose. Some were there serving as the muscle, some served as scavengers, and others served as researchers. The scavengers represented the most common members. They are the ones who would execute strong arms like theft, assist with attacking others to send a message, create opportunities for financial gain, and clean up various other problems. I was brought in for my craftiness and desire to succeed. Everyone had a purpose and each person helped make the whole group work to perfection. Big O liked the way I made a plan for everything. He liked how I created additional territory like with my "tick-tack" responsibilities and how I used my part time job to get business for the West DA Boy's car stereo business.

My new responsibility, as announced that evening, was to lead the "tick-tack" sales team and to get the numbers back up to where they were when I was producing. Having that responsibility placed on me was what I considered an initiation to becoming "The Man."

This power and respect was something my mom would never understand; therefore, it was best that I not inform her of my accomplishment. Without my family knowing, they would benefit from my position by receiving protection from the West DA Boys. With all the contacts favoring the West DA Boys, many families received protection. Although they never knew about such security, this was provided as a benefit because of their sons and brothers being members.

That night I got a real education about my new family. The only reason they knew about me being busted and where I was being held was because of their highest connections, known as "The Powers That Be." There are people everywhere who represent the West DA Boys. Remember, everyone in the gang has a purpose. As a West DA Boy, once you reach an age past adolescence and juvenile, you become a hidden asset. There are professionals such as doctors, lawyers, accountants, police officers, and many others that represent the West DA Boys. These assets remain on the payroll and serve the gang to the best of their profession. Knowing all this explained why the West DA Boys were known throughout various cities. The West DA Boys were more than what a common gang was; they were an enterprise. This information also added more pressure to what I was striving to do and to become.

That night I started organizing a plan to guarantee the success I was looking for and the leadership Big O expected of me. I was going to make the "tick-tack" business even greater than when I was producing. I listed the various schools in the area and the guys that were responsible for each location. I wanted to set up the same game plan that I had. I wanted each guy to be attached with actual students at each of those schools. The students would set up the sales and our members would provide the product. This would make them feel as if they had power.

I gave them the responsibility of arranging who their contacts would be. They were instructed to find up to three contacts per school. I also gave them the responsibility of expanding into newer areas by recruiting additional contacts to work just like the contacts they had within the various schools.

I was excited with how my weekend ended. It started off with me being released from a juvenile facility, my mom picking me up and treating me to some great soul food, reuniting with my siblings, getting crushed by my mom's news about being kicked out of the house, to being accepted into the West DA Boys and being given a great responsibility. Today was the day I got a step closer to becoming "The Man."

CHAPTER 15

TICK-TACK DRAMA

Getting back into the game was somewhat easy. Getting others to accept my plan on increasing sales and territory, posed more difficulty. The guys were always use to actually setting up their own deals and providing the products themselves. The combination of managing and providing for others efforts was new for them; however, it was this formula that created the success that I achieved. Although I never graduated from high school, I knew business was all about supply and demand, which boils down to products and profits.

For about two years, I led the team with the same mental goal in mind. Although we made a great deal of money, I still felt we could do more. We were the only ones in town offering "tick-tacks;" therefore, we had a monopoly on the product. With such a high demand for our product, if we execute business properly then we could feast on increased rewards long into the future.

One of the thoughts I had in reference to expanding into new territory, appeared to be a problem because another gang had claim to the areas in question. I was able to sit and meet with Big O to express a plan to capture new opportunities. He liked the idea I had so much, that he put an immediate call into "The Powers That Be." Before making a move like I was requesting, we needed to get approval. Big O was able to schedule a meeting where I would present a business perspective outlining everything I had discussed with him.

Although I've created my own adventures in the past, presenting a plan to "The Powers That Be" was different and very nerve wrecking. The level of these members represented exactly what I defined as "The Man!" Although I had one week to prepare my information, I was still responsible for business in our current areas. I needed to show the ability to have increased profits in our current situation in order to motivate "The Powers That Be" into accepting my suggestion for new growth.

As I began putting information together, Big O kept a tight watch over me. He needed to make sure that he understood everything I was doing because ultimately he would be held responsible. Although it was scary, I was motivated by the opportunity to speak to "The Powers That Be." This would be a chance for them to get to know who I was and why

Big O feels the way he does about me. This was an opportunity to separate myself from all the other West DA Boys.

While preparing for my presentation, two of my guys had an unfortunate encounter. They were jacked by the cops. While working their territory, three cop cars cornered them in the streets. Although this may appear to have been a negative for me, I would actually be congratulated due to prior changes I implemented. I made sure that my people were carrying lest than the legal amount of product allowed. I put this rule in place for such a situation like this. Even though we have contacts in multiple areas of the community, we still had to present ourselves as law-abiding citizens. I'm sure that the police officers knew exactly what was going on, but knowing and proving are two different avenues.

Although distribution dropped slightly in the areas my guys were busted in, by changing some demographics, profits were still good. The police were keeping a strong eye out on every move we made. One thing I learned in my quest to become "The Man," is that everything happens for a reason. If consequences or situations appear to be negative, then we can learn and build from them. Our ability to learn, build, and grow from experiences represent development.

With the difficulties I was facing in keeping our actions from the watchful eyes of the police, I also had an opportunity to prove to others that I was the right choice for this job. My desire and ability to overcome, would define me as the leader I know I am. With all eyes centered on me, increased accomplishments couldn't come at a better time. I was a shining star.

On the day of my presentation to "The Powers That Be," I knew this would be a major upward swing to achieving what I've long been looking for. Although my acceptance into power and leadership would anger a number of people within the West DA Boys, I could not care less. For those people who fail to advance from where ever they are, that's on them. I'm going to fight and get mine. To be honest, I could already feel the dislike that some members where having due to my fast upward growth.

Prior to my presentation, Big O and some of the other leaders in the gang, took me out for breakfast. This was the last opportunity for me to express to them the plan I created. I was asked questions they thought "The Powers That Be" would ask. The way I handled myself, was proof that I was more than ready. I responded to the guys in such a way that they too felt comfortable. Since the guys had been around "The Powers That Be" for some time, they had more of an idea of what that group would be looking for. As we finished practicing for the meeting, our pancakes were delivered to the table. The talk of business came to an end and we all pigged out.

We arrived at the meeting destination earlier than expected, which was perfect. The five of us remained in the car until we were instructed to come in. The other leaders, who were with Big O and me, were considered generals. I knew that before getting to Big O's level, the position of general was my next step. Even though such advancement takes time,

I wanted to be there yesterday. As we sat in the car, I noticed a number of well-dressed

individuals walking past us. Big O and the generals got out of the car to greet each one of

the individuals as they passed; however, I was told to remain inside.

Once all of "The Powers That Be" had arrived, I was escorted out of the car and into

the building. They had me sit in a waiting room until the group was ready to hear from

me. After about an hour, the doors were opened and I was asked to join the meeting.

Since this was my first opportunity to speak with "The Powers That Be," I knew I had

to show that I was intelligent, yet at the same time, I needed to represent the gang member

I was. Those guys, at one point in their lives, where hoods just like me; however, they

became the success they are because of their personal intelligence. There's no better way

for someone to advance than to show those who have control, that you too have the same

skills and abilities as they do.

After expressing gratitude for the opportunity given to me, I began to discuss the history

and growth of the product we called, "tick-tacks." I provided percentages that supported

its increase, both in profit and in territorial growth. I was able to show how developing

new territory increased the demand for our product. In any business, which "The Powers

That Be" represented through the West DA Boys, the higher the demand the greater the

opportunity for profit. Due to our diligence, we have saturated our current market. If we

want to keep growing, then we need to create new territory. Without developing new areas, in order to increase profits, we would have to increase cost, which would possibly decrease demand.

When it comes to business, an operation has three options: they can expand and grow, they can remain the same, or they can decrease and die. I believe if something remains the same, it will eventually decrease and die. Since the world is defined as always moving forward, then the only correct answer for us as an organization was to expand and grow. The only downside to my plan was that in order to avoid difficulties as we expand, we need to pay a service charge.

In any form of business, the desire to grow also means an increase in expenses; however, the hope is that the expenses are minimal compared to the profit opportunity. When given the responsibility to lead the operations of our "tick-tack" business, my main goal was to grow and build the entire team to be as successful as I was. Success comes from duplicating oneself into others and expanding the areas of production. As I came to the end of my presentation, the body language of everyone in room supported exactly how I was feeling. I knew that everyone understood what I was saying and that the picture I painted would bring about one answer.

After a long ten seconds, one by one, members representing "The Powers That Be" began to show their appreciation through applauds. The claps became louder as each one of them stood in agreeance. After the noise from the clapping died down, I was asked to leave the room while the fate of my presentation was discussed. I did not think there was much to talk about because everything was clear. It made sense and it left only one option available.

After about twenty minutes, I was asked to return into the room. Big O was standing in the middle of the meeting area and was asked to speak on behalf of those in attendance.

Once the announcement came out, it was obvious why they asked me to leave the room. Not only did they approve my presentation, but I was also named the newest general of the West DA Boys. "The Powers That Be" were so impressed with me, that they requested that I be promoted to the next level. I guess when it rains, it pours. I was truly becoming "The Man."

CHAPTER 16

UNHEALABLE WOUNDS

With all the good things happening for me, one would think that I had everything I wanted; however, I still felt one major void. There was a reason why I started doing all that I had done, yet the one person who was the center of my reasoning, had not accepted my accomplishments.

In order to decrease that void, I needed to give it one more try. I needed to get my mom to understand all that I had accomplished and let her know what drove me to such success. I understood how and why my mom felt the way she did, but I couldn't comprehend a parent giving up on their child. For someone who never finished high school to achieve the success I had, my mom should at least want to know and understand my motivation.

Occasionally, since before my arrest and even now, I would drop money off for my mom in the mailbox at her house. I would label it by writing, "I just want to help." There are also times when I would have a package delivered by UPS or any ground Delivery Company. Being able to help my mom made me feel like I was stepping up in the absence of my dad. With this most recent achievement, I felt it was time to sit with my mom and discuss everything, in reference to the how and why I did the things I did.

I chose a Sunday morning to confront my mom. It was traditional for her to go to church on Sunday and then go have lunch with some of the members. I parked outside her home and waited for her to return, which was normally around 2:00 o'clock in the afternoon. I waited a couple of houses down the street because I didn't want her to see me first and then drive off. Ever since she kicked me out, we really hadn't spoken; therefore, I wasn't only concerned about how she would react, but I was extremely nervous myself.

Just like clockwork, she came driving down the street heading home. As she pulled into the driveway, I slowly moved across from the house. I waited for her to go inside before I exited the car. I was still trying to deal with my fear of confronting her. Although it felt like I was sitting there for only a little while, it had actually been just over twenty minutes. I finally decided to get out of the car and approach the front door. Before I could ring the bell, the door opened.

"Well, how are you doing?" my mom said softly.

Hearing her voice made me feel like that little boy who was completely dependent upon his mom. I had to internally remind myself who and what I was. I responded to her by saying in a cool way, "All is good."

"I'm glad to hear that, so what brings you around here?" she asked.

I informed her that this wasn't the first time I came over. I told her that I've come around multiple times; however, this was the first time I came to talk.

"Come on in and have a seat," she said with an inviting and calm voice. "Before I can sit with you, I need to go into the back and get something of yours," she said as she closed the door behind me.

At first it felt strange walking back into my house, yet as I began to see familiar items it felt alright. When my mom returned, she sat on the opposite end of the sofa. I began to express the sadness and hurt I felt when my dad was gunned down. I told her that it was then, that I created my goal. I wanted to put myself at such a level that people would have great respect for me and that no intentional harm would ever come to me or my family. My goal was to do exactly what I'm doing now and that's to become "The Man!"

I admitted to some of the things that I had done to get to this point in my life. I talked about how I got started with selling candy bars and how that advanced into selling exams to other students. I did not talk about the "tick-tack" business because since it was illegal, I found that difficult for my mom to accept. Although I did quite a bit of illegal things, drugs would be a lot more difficult for her to accept. Besides, being a big wig in the "tick-tack" business also meant my mom could hurt the entire organization trying to teach me a lesson. I also talked about the car stereo business and about me getting arrested. As I expressed to my mom most of what I had done, she just sat there and took it all in.

I told her that everything I had done and was currently doing was fueled by my desires to benefit and protect our family. I also informed her that it was me, who was sending and leaving money in her mailbox. I wanted things to be easier for her because I knew the struggles she faced since my dad died.

After pouring out my heart, my mom sat in her seat frozen for about ten seconds. When she finally stood up, she walked over to where I was and gave me a big hug. As she hugged me, she whispered in my ear, "I love you." At that moment, I felt a huge weight lift off of my shoulders. I felt as if my mom finally understood why I did the things I did and was currently doing. Although she opposed those things, I truly believed everything was finally good again. During that brief moment, life was perfect.

When my mom sat back down in her original space, she began to express some things to me. "You talk about this image of becoming "The Man!" Honestly you don't even have a clue about what it means to be a man," she expressed.

Based on her facial expression and the tone of her voice, I could tell that this was not going to be as good as I had hoped it to be.

"I know you young boys think a man is someone who has the respect of hoodlums, gang members, and other juveniles of society, but that's not even close," she stated. "You see your manhood based on the number of females you've been with and the number of babies you've made, along with the money you've generated from your illegal activities. That's not being a man, that's nothing, but a negative statistic. Although your father died too early, it wasn't because of his own doing. Living life the way you are, it's almost guaranteed that it will end early by one of two ways, either in jail, which you've experienced or by being murdered."

Since I wasn't a little kid anymore, I tried to interrupt my mom, but she cut me off and kept right on going.

"I listened to you while you were speaking and while you spoke for the past few years, but now it's time for you to listen to me," she said as she halted my attempt to speak. "The life you're living, it's all about the products you have. Based on a sorry way of thinking, you think a man is defined by the money he has, the cars he drives, the number of women he's associated with, and even the number of babies he produces. Those things don't make you a man. Your father was "The Man." A true man is a man regardless of the clothes on his back or the size of the house he lives in," she said as tears began to run down her face.

I figured she began to feel emotional because she was talking about my dad. As she whipped the tears from her eyes, she continued. "A real man is someone who's an example of goodness, kindness, and love," she stated as her voice began to lower, bringing her point directly at me. "A real man makes the things around him shine, not the other way around. When we come into this world, we're naked and we have nothing, just like when we leave. A real man is someone, who between those two periods of time, makes their surroundings better through their actions and the lessons they provide for those they encounter and finally leave behind."

As she paused for a brief second, she reached under the table and grabbed a brown bag that she had brought from the room when I first arrived. She handed the bag to me and said, "I knew it was you who had been leaving money. I understand you felt that you were doing a good thing by helping me, but as much as I needed the money, I couldn't accept it. If I were to have taken this money, then that means I would be condoning the things you did to get it. How can I expect you to believe the things I'm telling you, if I allowed you to experience the benefits of being that bad version of what I just described?"

My mom then walked over to the door, as the tears started running down her face once again. As she opened the door, she gave one last bit of information to me, "Life is about making choices and a real man understands and accepts the struggles to making the right choice. Until you reach that point in your life, I can't be a part of you or your money. I truly love you, but I'm going to have to ask you to leave once again," she said as she bowed her head in discuss of what I'd become. There was nothing left for me to say, so I took the bag and left.

CHAPTER 17

MESSAGE DELIVERED

The drive away from my mom's house was a difficult one. It was just as bad as when she kicked me out for the first time. The only difference was that I currently have a lot more going for myself. I heard and understood all the things my mom said, but the hardest thing to accept was her expression of not wanting to be a part of my life.

Considering the fact that I do not have a father anymore, I was arrested, and I did not finish high school, my mom still could not accept all that I had accomplished. I am a great business man! I may not be wearing a tie and a suit, but I am a great creative thinker and a motivated achiever. I produce just as much money as any of those employees on Wall Street. Knowing and understanding that about myself, encourages me not to let her words hinder me. I am going to use those words as motivation to help me continue to fight and make my dream of becoming "The Man," a reality.

Instead of heading back to the hangout, I got right back to work. I went to the furthest location and worked my way back towards the hangout. My responsibilities were to check up on all the West DA Boys who were selling our "tick-tacks." One by one, each site was doing great. Even the newest sites in our most recently established territories were increasing in product sales. Everything was going well and of course that made me feel better about my life, compared to the way I was feeling when I left my mom's place. As our work day came to an end, which was around midnight, I was able to give a positive report to Big O. My positive reports made him, as well as "The Powers That Be," extremely happy.

The next few weeks went as smoothly as expected, until one day, one of my people in one of our newest territories called me with a rival gang situation. When such things like this happen, we call upon our West DA muscle. As mentioned, in our organization we have people for every situation. Those who represented our muscle were generally football jocks or other athletic participants. That evening, we sent five members, with three additional as back up, to deliver a response. Their responsibility was to send a message of our disapproval towards what had happened. Needless to say, they confronted the rival individuals and left a lasting message. A message was anything from a terrible beating to killing someone. We very rarely had to use the killing option because everyone knew and feared the West DA Boys. Normally, when we left a message, it was understood and that was it; however, this was a new day and time.

The very next evening, another message was left, but this time it was for us. One of our guys was found in the bushes at his distribution site with a bag of "tick-tacks" in his mouth. The rival gang responded to our response with the loudest of all responses, which was death. We immediately shut down all operations and began to organize ourselves for war. Since this was my first experience of battle, I took a back seat and played the role of a follower, instead of the leader I was promoted to be. Although I was extremely nervous about this situation, the West DA Boys were family to me, so I was motivated to fight back. I looked at this as a learning and developing experience. I was cool with the physical fighting aspect of war, but as we were getting organized, it was about guns and other weapons of destruction. This of course made the situation a bit more frightening.

Big O spoke to "The Powers That Be" and they made the call on when we were to go in and flex who the West DA Boys truly are. We were instructed to close in on the rival's hideout from all four directions. Although some of their members would not be there, we would satisfy our goal at reminding them that the West DA Boys are king and that their disrespect was unacceptable.

Based on our knowledge of the neighborhood and the information we received from our lookouts, we knew that the gang gathered at their hideout around 10:00 o'clock at night. They had four guys on two different rooftops about a block away and another six guys patrolling the streets, keeping an eye out for any attacks. It was like a game of chess and we were the grandmasters. All look out people for gangs are heavily armed, so the only way to disarm them was to take them out. We timed our move accordingly, at exactly 11:00pm we initiated our attack. The four guys on the rooftops and the six on the streets were taken out first, all without any casualties to our own.

As we surrounded the rival gang's hideout, we quickly became believers that there's no such thing as a perfect attack. As we began to sneak up on the hideout, shots rang-out towards us. It turned out that the rival gang had a third set of lookouts on another rooftop.

"Attack!!!" Big O shouted.

Without hesitation we returned fire at the hideout. We continued to fire shots for about five minutes straight, until no more shots were being returned. By the time the shooting had stopped, the last two lookouts were found and dealt with. When all the smoke had cleared, there wasn't one soul from the rival gang left standing. Our plan was to send a message; however, our actions turned into the destruction of an enemy. Once we verified that all of our members were accounted for, we quickly fled the area and headed back to our home. As we departed the scene, the sirens of the police were screaming around the neighborhood.

A few of our guys took bullets, but nothing too serious. With all the adrenaline flowing through my body, I was shocked to see, that I was one of those who took a bullet. I was shot in the right arm. The pain started to kick in like something I never felt before. The bullet actually went straight through my arm, entering through the bicep and exiting straight

through. Nothing major was hit; therefore, the damage was minimal. All we did was clean it

up with soap, water, and peroxide, then put a wrap on it with ice to keep the swelling down.

The message we sent was greatly advertised; however, the media could not put

responsibility on anyone. The action was just defined as gang violence. Although blame

was never assigned, other gangs knew exactly what had happened. After a few short weeks

of carefully working our territories and keeping an eye out for both the police and other

rival gangs, business was back up and running. Due to our lack of attention to business

for a couple of days, the demand for "tick-tacks" was high. Our absence opened the

opportunity for higher profits, which is exactly what happened. This of course made "The

Powers That Be" extremely happy.

Although I would have a permanent mark on my arm from the gunshot wound, it

represents a mark of credibility. Knowing that, made the pain feel a little bit better. My

plan was to get a tattoo around it, to help draw more attention to it.

During the next few months, we had a high increase of young guys wanting to become

members of the West DA Boys. Our message was highly talked about throughout the

various communities, which opened a large opportunity for growth. The growth of more

members, meant the growth of more territories and profits. I was able to promote some

guys to higher levels, giving them greater responsibilities. Having additional levels under

me, made my actual physical work easier. The members that met with me provided the information I needed to pass along to Big O, which he in turned passed over to "The Powers That Be." I had the "tick-tack" business working like a well-oiled machine. We actually operated like a top Fortune 500 Company.

With all I had done and all that I had experienced, being a top leader of the West DA Boys was exactly what I needed, to becoming "The Man."

CHAPTER 18

LEADER LEVEL DECISIONS

As our gang continued to increase in size, the opportunity for problems did as well. On occasions, some of my financial reports were lower than normal. My first thought was that one of the new guys was skimming money. Since the other guys had been working with me longer, I didn't think that they would be the ones causing this problem. I guess it was easier to accuse a stranger before accusing a friend. The only good thing was that my other locations where making so much more than usual, that it helped cover the difference from the lower area. This also gave me time to find a solution to what I was experiencing.

Although we kept track of the "tick-tack" bags, I needed to pay a little more attention to what was going out with each person. The way things worked, my head guys were responsible for gathering bags and giving them out to the lead guys under them, who then were responsible for giving bags to the team under them. As each work day ended, the process went in reverse. As my head guys turned in the remaining bags from the day, my reports were created. I had six head guys, who distributed bags to twelve lead guys, who then distributed bags to teams containing eight to ten guys. Somewhere between the going out and coming back in process, bags and money didn't figure out. Early on in my responsibilities, I changed the amount of bags each person carried; however, they all had secret spots to hide their bags until needed. I did that based on the additional coverage the police had focused on us.

As I made my daily rounds throughout our territories, I started speaking to each individual team member, getting their beginning balance. Sometimes I even got their mid-day balance as well as their ending balance. I didn't inform the guys above them what I was doing, because I didn't want anything to change until I figured out what was going on.

Almost three weeks passed and my calculation problems were still occurring. Finally, I had to test my head guys. I just knew it couldn't be one of them because they had been with the West DA Boys just as long as or longer than I had been. Some of the guys had been promoted by me; therefore, I felt nothing would come about from checking their numbers. Even though I would have never accused any of those guys, the facts supported something different.

I did not have to ask them the same questions I asked the members under them because their bags came directly from me. It took less than a week for me to uncover the criminal act from one of my head guys. Not only was money being skimmed, but as I presumed, bags were coming up missing as well.

This would appear to be a tough decision, since the culprit was a friend, but I had to remember that the West DA Boy's business was serious. My next move was to either confront the guy or rat him out to Big O. If I confront the guy, then the blood would be on my hands as well, because I was in charge; therefore, responsible. This is if anyone above me recognized the same calculation errors. The only way I could clear myself, was to take the information directly to Big O.

When I approached Big O, he explained to me, "With all that you have, you know what's in the best interest of the West DA Boys. One of our own stole from me, he stole from you, and he stole from our family. He has betrayed us; therefore, he has chosen his own fate. The only question is, are you willing to make that call?" Big O asked.

Big O's words made a lot of sense. It was my duty to continue to keep the family we've created. To allow this criminal act to go on was like me actually doing the act myself. The very next night as the guys were bringing their reports to me, I expressed the unjust activities that I uncovered. I made it clear that these actions were unacceptable and that the West DA Boy's would not tolerate such disrespect. After those words, without hesitation, I pulled my gun on the accused and shot him where he stood. As a general, this action was a sign to the other guys that we work as one and if anyone steps out of line, death was the consequence. It was tough for me to do what I had done, yet it was a necessity. Although I felt bad for my friend, I had honor and respect for my family.

Both Big O and "The Powers That Be" congratulated me on my decision. They said that I represented true leadership and dedication to our organization. My actions became well known, not only in our organization, but throughout the neighborhood. Due to these actions, I became feared by many. When my guys came together to give their reports, everyone was on time and no one came up short.

I liked the perception people had of me, but in this business, revenge is a great reason to worry. My worries were about someone trying to take me out for the decision I made against one of our own. I wasn't too worried about someone from our group because this was their family as well, but more so about those from other gangs. I even thought about non-gang related individuals who may have been close to that individual.

There is an old saying that states, "For every action, there's a reaction." The only thing is that we don't necessarily know when the reaction is going to occur.

With my newly found perceived power, I began to push the envelope, because of course I wanted more. I didn't only want to be feared because of what I did, but I wanted my appearance to be just as intimidating. I began to spend hours each day in the gym, pumping iron and doing a high level of cardio work. My workout regimen was two hours every morning and one hour at night. At first it was a struggle, but once the results started to show, I became a workout monster. In order to keep up with my workout schedule, I started indulging in a variety of substances to provide additional energy and a more visible physical outcome. These substances were taken either orally or through injections. As much as I hated needles, the necessity outweighed my fear.

After about six months, I looked like a sculpted work of art. My legs were like those of an NFL running back. My thighs were like metal pipes tide together and my calves looked like an inverted step. My stomach was a washboard eight pack topped with two solid rocks for a chest. My arms and shoulders had every muscle definition possible; biceps, triceps, forearms and much more. My look was so intriguing that other members started working out just as rigorous as I did.

Compliments from "The Powers That Be" continued to flow down, due to my examples and my leadership. They expressed that my dedication and commitment to our organization was exactly what they wanted all our members to resemble.

As I continued to receive complements from "The Powers That Be," from Big O and other members, it pushed me to work even harder. Everything appeared to be working out for me. My physical body was the best it had ever been and my leadership with responsibilities to the West DA Boys was at its highest level. It was safe to say that I was well on my way to achieving my ultimate goal of becoming "The Man."

CHAPTER 19

NEW RANKING

Our organization was working like a well-oiled machine. The "tick-tack" business was growing by leaps and bounds. Our car stereo business, as well as other endeavors, were making record profits. "The Powers That Be" were extremely excited about what was going on from a business point of view. Due to their excitement, many benefits rolled down hill to us, the workers.

With the popularity of our organizations actions, the door was opened for a higher level of harassment from the cops. As negative as the harassment may seem, it did keep us all on our toes. Each arrest gave way to about two days in a holding cell before being released. Nobody talked and nobody got caught red handed with an illegal amount of product. All cases were reduced to hearsay, which is why our members were held for no more than forty-eight hours. Hearsay is not strong enough to hold up in any courtroom, so all of our members learned to stay quiet as the police did their thing.

In the past, when we wanted to expand into a new territory, we made financial deals; however, with our growth and development we no longer had to make any kind of deals. If we wanting something, then we just took it by strong-arming the competition. In other words, if we wanted anything, like more territory, then we forced our way into it. As stated earlier, we did not have to kill much to make a point; sometimes a good beating was all it took to make a strong enough statement.

As great as it was to have created such fear and respect in others, the downside was that it opened the door for laziness. A few times, we did experienced such laziness, but after redeeming ourselves with a strong statement, we put things back in order. At least we thought things were back in order.

One Friday evening, about twelve of us went bowling. Generally, whenever we went out, we were very respectful; therefore, others were respectful towards us. On this one particular occasion, two guys began harassing our group. They singled Big O out and began bad mouthing him. We didn't pay much attention to them at first because maybe they had been drinking or they didn't really understand who we were.

As Big O was completing the tenth frame of his game, he accidently threw his bowling ball in the gutter. The two guys continued to joke about him even louder. Some of our guys jumped up and made remarks back, since ignoring them wasn't working too well.

Besides, we are the West DA Boys and we're not going to let anyone treat us as those jerks were doing.

Eventually, as we started to stand up for our leader, the two guys backed down and walked away. As they left, they flashed us the universal finger and shouted their gang name. Immediately when we heard they were associated with a gang, Big O instructed us all to leave. Everything felt like a set up and we only had twelve guys. We didn't worry about finishing our game or turning in the balls and shoes, our goal was to get out as quickly as possible before the set up could occur.

As we made it out to the cars, we were encouraged and thought all was good, but how wrong we were. Just as we got the car doors opened, gunshots came from every direction. Even though most of us got hit, we were able to still move and actually get into the cars. As we tore through the parking lot, bullets continued to penetrate our windows. We were able to get a good number of shots off as well, but we had no clue of where the shooters were located. As we got out of their range of bullets, Big O realized that he had been hit in the neck. Blood started squirting out of him like a fountain. Many of us were bleeding, but nothing was as bad as what Big O was dealing with. It was obvious that Big O was dealing with s a serious injury, so one of the generals quickly placed a call to "The Powers That Be."

As we arrived at the emergency facility that "The Powers That Be" instructed us to go to, Big O passed out. We actually carried him to the front desk, where the staff took him from us on a gurney. Since we called "The Powers That Be" before arriving, the staff was ready for us when we got there.

The staff asked no questions and no information was provided on what had happened. While the doctors worked on Big O, other nurses spent their time patching up the minor injuries on the rest of us. After about an hour of being at the medical facility, I and the three other generals were called into a meeting area with some of "The Powers That Be" that had arrived.

They showed up without our knowledge, which meant that something might be wrong. They met us in a private room. The meeting lasted no longer than ten minutes. We were instructed to clear out of the medical facility and head home. We were ordered not to do anything as a sign of revenge against the group who caused this situation. "The Powers That Be" said they would get in touch with us in the morning.

As we all drove off, our concern was about Big O. "The Powers That Be" couldn't give us any information and the doctors hadn't expressed anything either. Once we arrived back at the hangout, nobody was able to sleep. We all just sat around the house eager to know what was going on with our leader. Although we were instructed not to seek revenge, they didn't say we couldn't talk about it. For the rest of the night, that became our topic of conversation.

We made sure that we all remembered what the two individuals who set us up looked like. One guy was about six foot three, with a bald head, no glasses or facial hair, and about 225 pounds. Other guys talked about the tattoos on his arms and neck. The guy appeared to have an islander accent and wore a lot of jewelry. The guy who appeared to be in charge was about five foot ten, 200 pounds, a short afro, with a light mustache. He too had tattoos on his arms and neck, but not as much jewelry. We assumed he was in charge because he initiated the joking.

We started suggesting some revenge strategies that we could execute to keep up with our reputation. That gang delivered the greatest attack we have every experience; therefore, our revenge would have to be more than just standing up for the West DA Boys. Our revenge had to represent the honor of our leader, Big O.

Time passed quickly and before we realized it, the morning had come. Shortly before eight o'clock a call came in from "The Powers That Be." They informed us that they would be at our location within the next hour, so we needed to make sure that everyone would be in attendance. Before any questions were asked about Big O, the call was dropped.

We quickly made sure that the hangout was presentable for the arrival of "The Powers That Be." Even though we are gang members, we had great respect for our leaders; therefore, we refused to let them see the house they provided, in a messy light. We swept the floors, cleaned the counters and tabletops, emptied the trashcans, put toilet paper in all the bathrooms, picked up clothes, and prepared snacks. I think we worked harder than any mom on a Saturday mornings when cleaning the house.

As the convoy of cars came driving up the street, one of our lookouts contacted us about the arrival of "The Powers That Be." As they entered into the house, they quickly asked for a private meeting with the same group they met with at the hospital, which was myself and the other three generals. Instead of us going into another room, we stayed and everyone else was instructed to go outside and wait. I can't speak for the other guys, but I know I was freaking out. The meeting lasted for no more than twenty minutes. The statements made were both exciting and shocking at the same time. Before I and the other generals were able to ask questions and take in what had been passed down to us, the rest of the gang was called back into the house.

Once everyone was in the house one of "The Powers That Be" spoke. He announced to the gang about the death of Big O. A shock of silence went throughout the West DA Boys. Guys were angry about what was said and many of us had to fight back certain emotions. The big concern was about what was going to happen moving forward. All night we discussed what we wanted to do to honor our leader and how we planned to execute various strategies. The strange thing was, in creating those plans we never figured Big O would be dead.

Even though I was hearing this news for the second time, it was still very heavy to accept, but we all had to find a way. As sad as that information was, the next bit of news straightened me up and turned my world around. It was expressed to the entire gang that I was selected as the next head of the West DA Boys. In other words, I had finally achieved my goal of becoming "The Man!!"

CHAPTER 20

REVENGE

Although "The Powers That Be" saw fit to name me as the new head of the West DA Boys, not everyone was as excited as I was. Since there were three other generals and each one of them had been a member long before me, I'm sure each one of them would have preferred themselves in this position. One of the pressures I faced, like in any organization, was my responsibility to lead for the benefit of the entire group and not just for those who favored me.

As the new leader, one of my first desires was to provide some form of payback to the guys who eliminated our friend. Being successful with that endeavor would surely be a great start to increasing favor from those who may not have approved of my being in charge. In order to carry out such a task, I needed to first get the approval from "The

Powers That Be;" therefore, I had to come up with a plan on how to make this revenge attack work.

Within a couple of days of speaking and meeting with our guys, a plan was created. This plan would be a guarantee for upholding the honor of Big O and the entire West DA Boy's organization. Although this was a plan we all came up with together, I waited before presenting it to "The Powers That Be" because we needed to make sure that our current businesses were back on track. The other guys agreed with me; therefore, everyone stepped up to make sure we were doing what needed to be done.

After about a month, our business with the car stereos and "tick-tacks" were better than ever. We regained control of our existing territories and increased production by just over 20%. We were also able to secure additional areas. I constantly received messages of congratulations from "The Powers That Be" because of my leadership and motivation at getting our members back on track. All of this was done while still dealing with the loss of our previous leader and friend.

Since I shared, what was provided to me from "The Powers That Be" with all our members, my approval rating was on an upswing. Guys began to favor me as their leader and our increased results was supported by their actions. With everything moving in the right direction, I felt it was time to request the approval from "The Powers That Be" to execute our revenge plan.

Late one Tuesday evening, we were having our newly created bi-weekly meeting. It consisted of "The Powers That Be," myself, and the generals of the West DA Boy's. With the increase in business, the meeting was pleasing and uplifting. As the meeting began to near an end, I respectfully requested additional time so we could discuss the matter of getting revenge for the death of Big O. "The Powers That Be" appeared to be aware of what was coming. Before I could say another word, one of them shouted out, "why now?"

I expressed how the thoughts of revenge never left any of us. I talked about the great impact that Big O had on our growth and development at becoming the organization we are today. The most important concern I expressed was that our enemies know what happened and it was up to us to remind them that no one messes with the West DA Boys.

"You have shown great leadership in motivating your colleagues to get back to work and to generate the increased numbers you've provided for us earlier," one of "The Powers That Be" expressed. "We all agree with the direction you've chosen to take and we're grateful to you, but what good is getting revenge. People come and go, but at the end of the day it's all about the business and from the looks of things, business is great."

I responded by expressing how revenge would provide additional motivation. I explained that the gang was working on autopilot, yet everyone still had a great concern for the loss of our leader and friend. I also made it clear that we as leaders are doing all we can to execute the success they wanted and desired from us. I ended by stressing that revenge would serve as a great motivator in keeping the wheels spinning.

"If we move forward with this revenge program, what's to stop another attack from mounted against us?" one of the powers asked.

Although we understood the vicious cycle of gang revenge, I told "The Powers That Be" we were willing to take that chance. Before revealing our plan, I expressed that we were unclear on why such an act was aimed at us in the first place. Our plan was to find out more about who performed this cruel act and to get every bit of information possible about them before moving forward. We wanted to know more about them than we knew about ourselves. Once we had a handle on all the information needed, we would strike in silence. When all the dust clears, the only thing left behind would be victims and mystery. The attack would be similar to the response we delivered a few years ago.

"Get all the information you can, then come back to us and we'll revisit the revenge idea then," one of the powers stated.

As the meeting ended, I spoke with the other generals and arranged a meeting for all the West DA Boys back at the hangout. We needed to confirm our plan on how to gather what we needed in order to get the approval of operation "Silent Night." We came up with the name because it defined what we were trying to do. The enemy would never see us coming and when all was done, no one would be able to define who do it.

Our plan to get the information we needed was to assign some of our newer and younger members to undercover duties. They were to hang out at the bowling center where everything initiated and look for the two guys that started our nightmare. Once they found them, then they had to follow them and find out who they are representing and where they were located.

After about three weeks, we finally got word that the two guys were spotted playing pool at the bowling center. The two guys were new to the neighborhood and their initiation into the city's local gang, the Northside Saints, was to set up the West DA Boys. The gang was known as a small time organization who committed crimes like breaking in and robberies. They were best known as an annoyance rather than a serious threat. Their actions against us was an attempt to upgrade their image. Our guys followed them for about a month before we felt we had enough information to revisit with "The Powers That Be."

When we eventually met with "The Powers That Be," the approval was given and operation "Silent Night" was a go. We learned that "The Powers That Be" also wanted revenge for the killing of Big O; however, their primary concerned was about continued business. This organization has been around for a long time and members come and go. Doing what we do brings about death; therefore, "The Powers That Be" have to focus more on the long-term business, not individual matters. That is how the game is played.

The movements of the Northside Saints were simple and repetitive. On Friday's, during the early evening, they played basketball at Northside Park, which was where they hung out most days. Their hideout was a rundown house about two blocks south of the park with a variety of escape routes, which would be beneficial for us. They had three lookout points with two people in each and their gang consisted of about thirty to thirty-five members.

A group that size would be no match for someone like us because we were over seventy members strong.

We decided to execute operation "Silent Night" on the first Monday morning of the month. The reason why we selected Monday morning was because the Saints had a standing meeting every Sunday evening. Afterwards, they would party together as a celebration for all the gang related activities they accomplished the prior week. We also selected that time because it was the best opportunity to catch the highest number of them together.

Our plan was to take out the six guys who worked the lookout spots first, then go in to tear down and destroy the rest of the gang while in their house. By destroying everyone, we would eliminate the opportunity for witnesses and the ability for additional actions against us from this group. The plan was just like our message to the rival gang that took out one of our members and stuffed "tick-tacks" in his mouth; however, this time we planned for any surprises.

Our schedule was to initiate our operation at exactly 1:30 in the morning. We figured by that time the guys would be less conscious and alert from the effects of their partying. Many of them might even be passed out, which would make "Silent Night" even more successful.

On the afternoon prior to our revenge day, we all gathered at our hangout. I took that time to motivate, encourage, and re-educate the gang on the importance of what was about to go down. I stressed the importance of what Big O did for our organization and how disrespectful the Northside Saints were for attacking us and taking his life. Other individual also took the opportunity to express their feelings about Big O and his contributions. When all was said and down, each member had exactly what they needed to go out and execute operation "Silent Night" and make it the success we all dreamed about.

We left the hangout at 10:00 that Sunday evening, just as we planned. We had three groups of four guys who were responsible for the three lookout spots of the Northside Saints. As the time came for us to initiate our attack there was no turning back. Once we confirmed the lookouts were down, the rest of us would surround the house and the attack would be on.

As the clock struck 1:30, our guys eliminated the two lookouts at each of the three spots. Now it was up to the rest of us to finish the revenge attack. As we approached the house, you could hear music playing and the loud chatter from some of the guys who were still alert. The rest of them had partied very hard because they had passed out on the floor and in the various rooms of the house, which is exactly what we had expected.

I knew this was going to be like taking candy from a baby. On the same count, we broke into the house from all available doors and windows and began to spray bullets everywhere. When I say we handled our business, we did just that. Within five minutes, all was said and done. The job was done and we were out. We left just as quietly as we arrived. We suffered no casualties and left no knowledge of our existence. Operation "Silent Night" was a success and our revenge for our fearless leader was completed. I led the West DA Boys to victory, which in turned labelled me as "The Man."

CHAPTER 21

REALITY

After about five months from the completion and success of our operation "Silent Night," things have been running awesomely. All of the guys were extremely supportive of me and they were willing to do whatever I asked of them. Our businesses were at the highest levels they had ever been and our membership was growing by leaps and bounds. I was running and leading a highly feared and respected organization.

My goal of becoming "The Man," had finally come true. I was experiencing power, money, and the choice of any woman I wanted. I drove a fancy car with of course the best sound system available to man. I had the best of the best when it came to my bling and name brand shoes and sports apparel. I was greatly respected everywhere I went.

Life was great and at the age of twenty-four, I was sure to be experiencing this for a good ten to twenty years more. I never wanted to give up what I strove so long to achieve. I was serious about my leadership, but I played it safe by making sure I was well protected at all times. I didn't want the same thing that happened to Big O, to happen to me.

After about another year of high success, I noticed that my respect level had reached that of those who represented "The Powers That Be." As good as that felt, I still needed to remember and understand my place. I compared my responsibility to that of a star athlete. No matter how good the athlete is, the owner is still the head of the team. The rest of the staff and players are all employees. Once that star athlete forgets his responsibility, things begin to crumble. Although it's easier said than done, the respect and acknowledgements from others can push a person to think that they're more than they really are.

In my mind, my importance to the West DA Boys was irreplaceable. No matter how successful things were, while under the leadership of Big O, my accomplishments put me far ahead of him. My ego became so large that at times I even questioned certain decision made by "The Powers That Be."

We were experiencing a situation in one of the areas where we had expanded. Our "tick-tack" business was growing at a rate unheard of since we began this operation. "The Powers That Be" suggested we slow down the business in that particular region. In my mind, business runs a course, it's either good or it's bad. When it is good, you ride that horse until it bucks you off, but when it is bad, you slowdown and make changes.

In reference to the area in question, business was awesome; therefore, it did not make sense to slow things down. Due to my lack of understanding and personal pride, I went against the request of "The Powers That Be" because I needed to prove them wrong. I continued to expand our business in that particular region, because I needed to defend the fact that "I'm The Man!" Knowing this was a risky move, it made all the sense in the world to me. Sometimes individuals do things against the suggestions of authority, but when it works out, there are usually great benefits.

Just as I predicted, our business continued to increase. Our profits became unspeakably high. The success of my actions showed the West DA Boys that I was on top of my game as their leader. The support of the gang overwhelmingly began to follow my thoughts and decisions over those of "The Powers That Be."

Life couldn't be any better than what I was experiencing at that point and time. My leadership with the gang and with our businesses greatly supported the fact that I was the right choice for the job. I had proven myself to "The Powers That Be," to the other gang members, and most importantly, to myself. I was highly thought of and shown respect by those both of gang affiliation and those without. It was safe to say, as I did often to myself, "I'm The Man!"

About another six months had passed and the West DA Boys were having continued success in every aspect of business; however, it was then that I experienced one of the worst days of my life. While having a late breakfast at a small neighborhood diner with three of my generals, we witnessed about five cop cars racing down the street with sirens blaring. All five cars stopped in front of the diner. Immediately, one of the generals told me to escape out of the back door. They all sat at the table as a distraction for the cops as they entered into the diner. Once I reached the back door, another three cop cars were there surrounding the exit.

"Freeze!" One of the officers yelled, as I tried to run back into the diner. "If you move, we'll be forced to open fire," the same office expressed.

I didn't know exactly what was going on, but I remained calm as the officers placed me under arrest. We've always been instructed by "The Powers That Be" to always respect and obey the officer when in a situation like I was experiencing, then when an opportunity presented itself, call them first.

As the cops handcuffed me and placed me in the back of a squad car, I realized my three generals were let go. This was strange to me because I'm sure the officers knew they were with me. As the leader of the West DA Boys, it would be unheard of for me or any other leader to travel alone, so why didn't the other guys get arrested too? This question haunted me as the cops drove me to the station.

When we arrived at the police station, I was quickly booked and placed in a holding cell. I continued to be respectful because I knew my opportunity to make a phone call was coming soon. Once I was able to make my call, I knew things would get taken care of. The problem was, that opportunity never came. Although I asked for the chance to make a phone call, the officers kept saying I'd get that call later. I figured they were just trying to be difficult with me, so I didn't worry too much. In my mind, there was no need to worry because I was sure that the gang and "The Powers That Be" knew exactly where I was and that they would be coming to rescue me as soon as possible.

While sitting in the holding cell, after a few hours had passed and no information had come about anyone looking for me, my mood began to change. I became angry with the entire organization. After all the things that I had done for the West DA Boys, how could they forget about me? I was like the Michael Jordan of our organization, I was "The Man!"

As I set in the holding cell for just over a day's time, no one had communicated about what was actually going on. The only thing I knew was that I was going into court within the next couple of days. I tried to remain positive, although I was angry. To be honest, my thought was, there was no way "The Powers That Be" would not be there for me. Maybe they were working on a defense for my case and they weren't given access to me because of how the system works. Maybe the system was blocking any communication from the outside because they were trying to set me up. So much was going through my mind that I could not really think straight or even understand what was truly happening.

Finally, the long awaited moment had come. An officer came into the cell to escort me to the courtroom. When I walked in, the normal legal representation for the West DA Boys was not there. The court had given me someone from their office. As I looked into the audience, I realized that there was no one there from "The Powers That Be" or from our gang. I was on my own. It was then that I started to realize the reality of what was happening. I was being set up, but not by the officers who arrested me. I was being set up by my own organization, the West DA Boys and "The Powers That Be."

As I continued to scan the audience, familiar faces appeared to me. I was truly shock when I saw the individuals, but it made sense. It was my mother, my brother, and my sisters. Although my mom loved me, she admitted many times that she didn't support what I was doing, yet she and my siblings were the only ones there for me. I hadn't spoken to any of them in over two years and now my only comfort came from those I personally shunned away from.

As the judge read the charges, I finally realized what I was being accused of. It was me who directed the destruction and murder of multiple people, which was our "Silent Night" operation. It was me who was responsible for the distribution of the "tick-tack" drugs. As a third strike, it was me who was involved in multiple counts of auto theft. Of course all of these charges were true; however, I didn't do any of them alone. All the pieces of the puzzle became clear. This was payback from "The Powers That Be" to show that I was never "The Man."

When I started doing things against their request and leading as I saw fit, they needed to regain their authority. Due to their high connections, I was the lamb to the slaughter. "The Powers That Be" were responsible for my never seen before lawyer as well as the arrangement of the judge presiding over my case. By putting all these accusations against me, it closed the books on current investigations by the police. It also opened the door to continued opportunities for the West DA Boys.

All that I had done to become "The Man" was for nothing. I developed the highest profits ever for "The Powers That Be," and I climbed to the top of a well-known and powerful organization. I did all this by gaining the support and honor of its members, yet in the end it all meant nothing. My mom was right when she expressed what being a real man was truly about. In our last conversation she said a real man is an example of goodness, kindness, and love. She said that a real man fights to make the things around him shine. In other words, a real man is one who strives to make the world a better place. When all is said and done, what lessons have I taught and what examples have I left behind?

Throughout the entire trial, all I could think about was how I let everybody down; my family, my church, and all that was truly good in my life. My father provided so many positive examples for me, but I was angry and confused when the tragedy of his death occurred. I failed to have faith and trust in my upbringing; therefore, I saw life through things outside of my beliefs. Now that my situation is where it is, my eyes are open. If I could do this all over again, I would understand that I don't know everything and I'd listen more to those who truly love me.

After all the information had been delivered and the jury returned from their deliberations, the judge asked me to stand. I knew what was about to happen, so I tried my best to prepare my emotions as the jury leader read the verdict. I was found guilty on all accounts and it was requested that I be sentenced to death. As the outcome was being read, I turned back to look at my mom. She looked right into my eyes as tears ran down her face. It was then, at that point and time, that my emotions began to show.

The judge agreed with the findings of the jury and added that I would be sentenced to the electric chair. As the officers walked me out of the courtroom, my emotions had no filter. I cried like a baby because there was no more chances for me, even though I knew and understood where I went wrong. While walking out, I yelled an apology to my mom. I expressed to her that she was correct in what she said about being a real man.

Time stood still as I waited for that crucial day to arrive. While sitting in my cell, I kept reflecting back on when I went wrong. As a young man, we think we know everything; therefore, we make choices based on false imaginations. Although times have changed, as well as people, the game of life is still the same. Parents are there to direct us because they have more of an understanding about the game. Whether they played the game right or not, they've been through it; therefore, they're our best resources. We may still make mistakes along the way, but at least we have a better chance at winning when the game is over, if we just listen to the advice they give.

I knew the time was coming soon because I was asked what I wanted to eat for my last meal. Eating whatever I wanted always made me feel better about my situation. I requested both fried chicken and barbecue ribs, with some macaroni and cheese, corn bread, black eye peas, and peach cobbler for dessert. My food seemed to arrive faster than anything ordered at a restaurant. Although I was facing an unchangeable situation, food always seemed to make things a lot better.

As I ate my food, I thought back to the good times when our family would eat like this on Sunday's after church. Sometimes my mother would cook and other times we would go out as a family. Food is like the universal medicine and I ate so much that I was ready to take a nap once I finished.

Once they cleared away the remains of my meal, that moment had arrived. I was led to a room surrounded by about ten additional officers. I was unable to get emotional and there was no turning back. My fate had been secured and there was nothing I could do about what was happening. The result I was facing, was due to the choices I made a long time ago. As I was being strapped in the chair, I could see my family sitting on the other side of the glass. Once again, it was my mom, my brother, and my two sisters. Even until the end, they were still the only one's there for me.

Thinking back to when my father died, I always wondered why Christians, believers of God, or believers in anyone's spiritual higher being, allowed themselves to suffer so much in life. Being where I am now, it makes sense. In life, here is where we fight through the rough times, with the hope of experiencing great rewards spiritually. The greatest reward comes when all is said and done. It comes through those you leave behind and it comes in what believers define as the afterlife.

Experiencing this difficult situation, finally taught me the true meaning of life and what was important. My mom was right in all the things she tried to get me to understand, when it came to being a real man. If only I knew then, what I know now.

As the countdown began, the fight of holding back my emotions got tougher. "10...9...8...7," the officer counted. Tears started to run down my face. "6...5...4...3," the officer continued to count.

While strapped in this chair waiting to fulfill my punishment, the only hope going through my mind was for those coming after me. Although I messed up my life, hopefully others can learn from my mistakes. I don't have another opportunity, but many of you still do. The question is, knowing what you know now, from the advice given by those who have been through the game of life, what are you going to do about it?

"2...1" buzzzzzzzzzzzzzzz!!!!!

Printed in the United States
By Bookmasters